Snowbody Has To Know

Snowbody Has To Know

Seasons of Love Book Two

MICHELE ELIZABETH

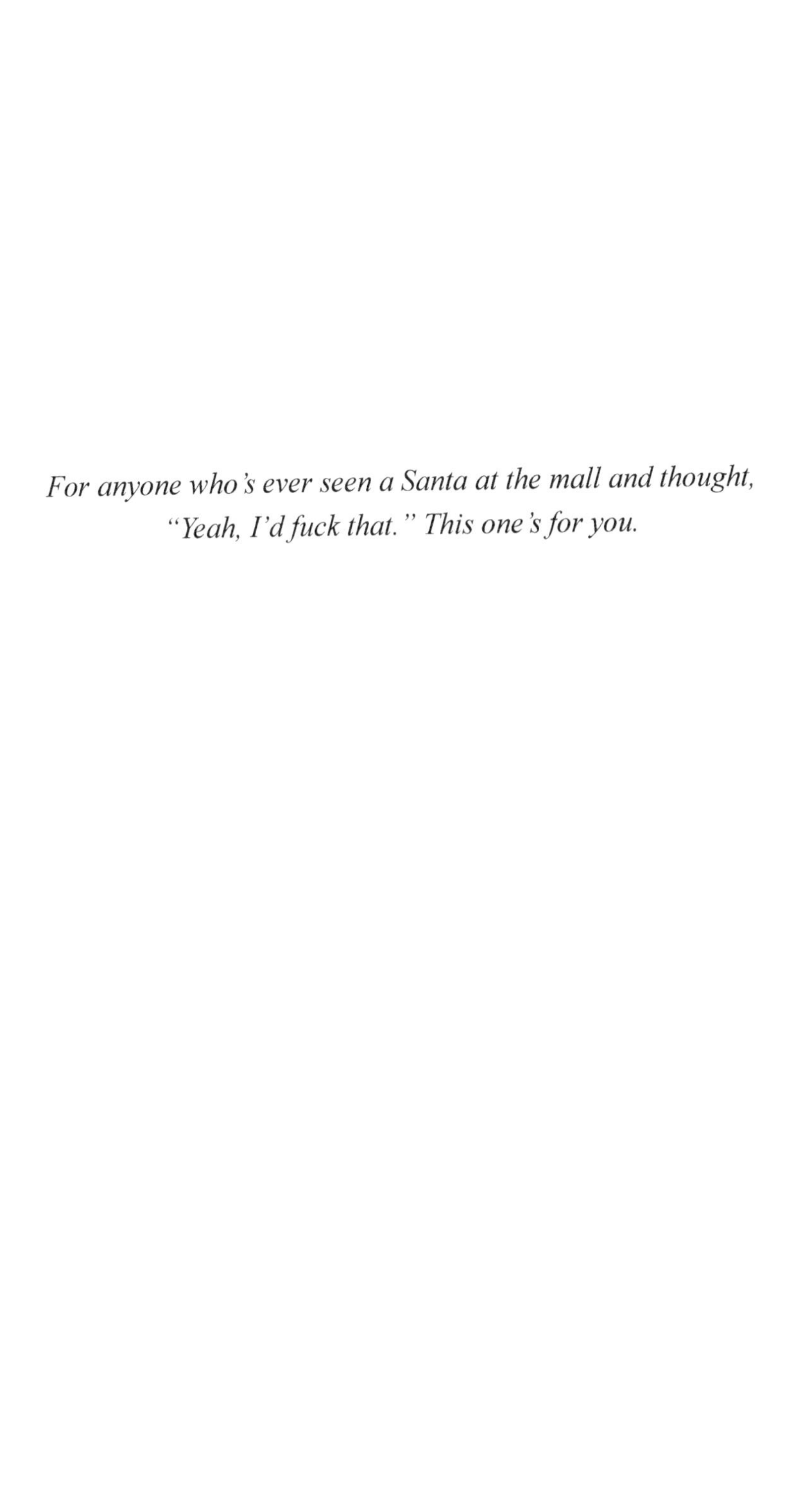

*For anyone who's ever seen a Santa at the mall and thought,
"Yeah, I'd fuck that." This one's for you.*

A NOTE TO READERS

Your mental health matters. This book is a fun, spicy holiday themed romance, but also touches on some heavier topics. For a full list of tropes and content warnings please visit www.micheleelizabeth.com/books

PLAYLIST

Craving snow, spice, and a little
seasonal swoon?
Check out the Snowbody Has To Know
Playlist on Spotify:

PROLOGUE
BRANDON

The club buzzed with excitement, and, oddly enough, so did I. Under normal circumstances, I wouldn't be caught dead at a busy nightclub for a Halloween party, but when Nathan asked me to play wingman, I was all in. He had been talking about this girl nonstop since meeting her a few weeks ago, and tonight was the night he was going to shoot his shot again. She had already turned him down once, but since then, he'd really been putting in the work to win her over. I was optimistic that he'd finally get the girl and excited to be a part of it. Usually, my brother Dylan would be the obvious choice for a night out at a club, but he thought this whole thing was stupid since he wasn't a fan of relationships.

I, on the other hand, was what you might call a romantic at heart. And even though I'd been unlucky in love so far, I wanted my brother to find his person. I knew from an early age that I wanted the kind of love my parents had shared.

Seeing them have fun, work together, and build an amazing life set the standard for what I wanted for my own life one day. Sure, I had dated, but I hadn't found my person yet. I thought maybe I had once, but she wasn't the one for me. I wasn't really looking for anything in particular; I didn't have a list or anything, but I always thought I'd just know when I met her. *Corny, I know.*

Nathan and I were leaning against a bar, taking in our surroundings, when my gaze landed on *her*. There was no way for me to actually hear her, but it felt as if I could when she tilted her head back and laughed with her whole body. That smile and the way she commanded attention—it was no wonder that a crowd of eager suitors had surrounded these two gorgeous women dressed as sexy clowns. Her friend, whom I assumed was Daphne because of her coordinating attire, was staring intently at my brother, whose face was now covered by his mask.

"Hey, is that them?" I elbowed my brother in his side.

He answered almost immediately. "That's her." Then he was gone, meeting her in the middle of the dance floor. They talked for a moment and then took off out of sight.

After watching them disappear, I looked back towards Daphne's friend, Lexi, who was now staring back at me. I told Nathan I'd keep her company while he and Daphne caught up, but what I didn't know at the time was that Lexi was fucking gorgeous. Even from across the club and in her ridiculous costume, I could tell that she was attractive. I couldn't tell her height or eye color from where I stood, but I found her curvy figure and the confidence she exuded sexy as hell. I smiled and raised my glass in her direction. She smiled back and then started towards me, swaying her hips the whole way. *Who knew I'd have a thing for clowns?*

"Hey, I'm Lexi. You must be Brandon." She stopped in front of me and held her hand out for me to shake.

"Hey, yeah. Brandon. Nice to meet you, Lexi." I took her hand in mine and gave it a squeeze. She was beaming up at me with a wide smile. Now that she was right in front of me, I could fully appreciate her beauty. She seemed to be of average height for a woman with a full figure, which made me want to drop to my knees right there to worship her. Her bright blue eyes and ample breasts fought for my attention, but I kept my shit together long enough to ask, "Can I get you a drink?"

"Yeah, thanks. I could use another vodka soda," she said as she came up next to me at the bar, placing her now-empty glass down while I flagged down the bartender.

Once I had secured fresh drinks for the both of us, I turned to her and held up my beer. "Cheers. To new friends."

"To new friends." She winked at me as she clinked her glass against mine and then took a sip. "So, how'd you get roped into this?" she chuckled.

"Honestly, it didn't take much convincing. I really hope this works out for them. I mean, what a way to meet!? What were the odds? It's like it was meant to be," I babbled. Lexi was so distracting, I wasn't even sure of what I was saying.

"Meant to be?" Lexi scrunched up her nose. "I don't

know about all that, but my girl deserves to be happy, and if Nathan makes her happy, then I'm here for it."

"So, I take it you don't believe in fate?" I asked.

"Ha! Not on your life! Every choice we make leads us to a future that we created, good or bad. It's not written in the stars or whatever. That shit only happens in movies." She rolled her eyes and continued, "You really think you have no say in your future happiness?"

"Well, no, that's not what I'm saying." She had me there. *Did I really believe our fates were predetermined?* This was some heavy shit for a first meeting.

She raised an eyebrow. "So what *are* you saying?"

"I guess I mean that it's hard to imagine their meeting at that cabin was some sort of coincidence. They both went through breakups, and just so happened to be at the same place at the same time? That's too crazy of a coincidence for me. Listen, I know we are all in control of our own choices, and those choices determine our futures, but when it comes to love and meeting your person, I guess I'm just a romantic. So sue me." I shrugged and took a swig of my beer. This wasn't the typical getting-to-know-you kind of conversation I was used to having. She was making me think, and I was actually enjoying our little back and forth.

Then she acted like she was throwing up, complete with exaggerated gagging and motioning to her mouth with her finger. "Um, no, thank you, sir. I am happily single and ready to mingle, and I plan on keeping it that way. Relationships are a fucking joke, anyway. They all end eventually, and someone always gets hurt. Hard pass. But good on you for being so emotionally available or whatever," she snorted. "I'm sure your girlfriend eats that shit up."

Mentioning my non-existent girlfriend seemed like a ploy to find out if I was single, but everything else she was saying seemed to contradict that. *There was no way she was interested in me, right?* Even though she clearly wasn't looking for a relationship, I couldn't help but entertain seeing where this would go. "No girlfriend, but I hope when I meet her, she's less of a skeptic." I laughed and took another sip of my beer.

"Skeptic? I prefer the term realist. But enjoy living in your fantasy world where everything always works out for you. Must be nice." She smiled sarcastically and then finished her drink. "If we are going to keep the conversation so serious, I'm gonna need another one of these," laughing, she held up her glass towards the bartender.

"I don't think I started it, but I got you." I put more cash down on the bar to cover her drink.

"What a gentleman. Thanks." She took a sip of her fresh drink and continued, "Okay, let's change the subject. So what is it you do for work, Mr. Romantic?"

I laughed, because what was I going to do? Refute the title? I was, after all, a hopeful romantic at heart, despite my past heartbreaks. "My brother, Dylan, and I run our family's tattoo shop here in the city."

"Oh, nice. I guess I should have known. I mean, look at you." She gestured in a sweeping motion towards my six-foot-four, mostly tattooed-from-neck-to-ankle body. One usually assumed I was either a tattoo artist myself or a criminal of some sort, a stigma that pissed me off, even if it was meant as a joke. "Oh, I've always wanted a tattoo. I've been begging Daphne to do bestie tattoos, but she keeps making excuses. I may have to go and pop my cherry without her."

"You'll have to come by the shop sometime. I'll hook you up," I offered with an involuntary wink. *Who was I?*

"Maybe I will. Thanks," her voice trailed off as she scanned the club. Her brows furrowed. "Oh, fuck no." Lexi's concerned expression had me following her line of sight, but before I could figure out what she was looking at, she was off and moving across the club.

I quickly pushed off the bar and followed her. I wasn't sure where she was going, but she looked pissed. Rounding a corner, I momentarily stopped in my tracks when I saw Nathan punching some guy in the face.

1

LEXI

One Month Later

"Oh, fuck, I'm coming," I moaned into his neck. I needed to let… *Shit, what was this guy's name?* Didn't matter. I needed to let him know I was done so we could get this over with. He was just another in a long line of dudes I wouldn't see again. He'd probably try to see me again, of course, but I wasn't interested. I wasn't what you'd call a relationship girlie. I was more of the 'fuck and run' type.

The man hovering above me grunted out his own release. *Time to make my escape.* "Damn, baby, that was so hot. You're wild," what's-his-name murmured into my neck.

"Mmm, yeah, that was great." I tried to sound as believable as possible as I extricated myself from underneath him. "But I've gotta get going. Got an early shift tomorrow." I hopped out of his bed, grabbed my clothes, and headed for the en suite to clean up.

He called after me, "Oh yeah, me too." *Yeah right.* I was all too familiar with this routine. Even if he wanted me to stay, which he didn't, he wouldn't ask because I beat him to the punch to make my exit. That was how my one-night stands usually went—we both got off *hopefully*—and then I went running for the hills: no strings, no repeats, no feelings. Well, maybe a repeat once in a while, but that was only when I was looking for a sure thing. This guy, though, was just another random I picked up at a bar for a good time. A girl has needs, you know, and if a guy can sleep around without consequence, why can't I?

I made quick work of getting cleaned up. What's-his-name sat up in bed when I returned to the bedroom and made like he was going to get up. "I'll walk you out," he said, pausing at the end because I was sure he forgot my name, too.

"No need. I'm good. See ya around." I gave him a small wave and then made my way to the living room, grabbed my purse, and got the fuck out of there. Thankfully, his place was pretty close to mine, so I could walk home.

As I got to the street and turned towards home, I pulled out my phone to see what Daphne was up to. I hadn't seen her in what felt like forever. In reality, she was still technically staying on my couch, although she spent almost every waking moment with her new guy, Nathan. And I mean, who could blame her? He was the total package and was hopelessly in love with her. She was one smitten kitten.

She answered right away, "Hey, hooker, what's up?"

"Funny you should use that word choice," I laughed. This bitch knew me so well. "Just leaving a rando's place, but I'm hungry and I wanted to see if you were around and wanted anything if I stopped?"

"Aren't you thoughtful? But I'm good. I'm actually at Nathan's and won't be home tonight."

"Color me shocked. You two are disgusting," I joked, making a puke sound.

"Don't worry, you're still my number one boo. Let's have a girls' night this week, okay?" Daphne was my closest friend and knew me better than anyone. She knew that while I pushed most people away, I also needed friend time.

"Okay, sounds good. We'll chat at work tomorrow. Love ya."

"Love you, too. See you tomorrow," Daphne replied.

We hung up our call as I walked into my favorite Chinese place. "Hey, Mei," I called to the girl working behind the counter. Her family had owned this restaurant for years, and she practically grew up working here; at least that's what I had learned. In my humble opinion, they had the best Chinese food in the city, and thankfully, they were conveniently within walking distance from my apartment.

"Hey Lexi, what can I get you?" Mei answered and moved to the register to ring in my order.

"Just the chicken lo mein for me tonight, thanks."

"Do you ever get sick of eating the same thing all the time?" Mei asked as she took my payment.

"Not when the shit is this good, girl," I answered truthfully.

She laughed. "Well, I'm glad you like it, and we always appreciate your business. It'll be a few minutes. Can I get you something to drink while you wait?"

"I'm good, but thanks." I moved to sit in a booth by the register and took out my phone. There was already a missed text from Daphne with a link to a tattoo shop.

DAPHNE

Bestie tattoos this weekend?

ME

Hell yes!

Sweet. Now I had something to look forward to this weekend, but right now, the priority was food, a shower, and sleep, in that order. After retrieving my order from Mei, I made my way home.

My second-floor walk-up apartment was in a decent part of the city, close to shops, work, and some wonderful restaurants and bars, too. It was the perfect spot for a single gal living her best life. And I was. My life was pretty great. I had a job I didn't hate, a best friend who would definitely help me hide a body and a nice place to lay my head at the end of a long day. Most people would say, "But what about a partner to share your life with?" To them I'd reply, "No fucking thank you." Love wasn't in the cards for me. I was totally okay being alone, and I'd rather be alone than have to deal with the aftermath of a failed relationship.

Growing up the only child of a single parent who pined

for her lost love was no picnic. Don't get me wrong, my mom was the freaking best mom I could've asked for. She was loving, kind, and fun to be around, and was always my friends' favorite too; the cool mom. She taught me to be a strong, independent woman and not to rely on a man to do things like changing a tire or patching some drywall. But there were many nights when she thought I was asleep or when she thought she was alone that I'd hear her crying. She wasn't the happy-go-lucky person she pretended to be. I think it was because she missed my dad. Although I don't really remember him, and she rarely spoke of him, I knew she had loved him and that one day he had just left us without a word. I didn't really blame him; I guess. He was a kid himself when my mom got pregnant at seventeen. They tried to make it work, from what I understood, but he couldn't handle the pressure and took off.

Some shrinks might say I have daddy issues, or whatever, and that's why I sleep around, and maybe I do. But I have zero desire to get close enough for anyone to hurt me like my mom got hurt. Sure, my dad leaving probably messed me up, too, but seeing the effect it had on her did me dirty, and I'd be damned if I let any man do that to me. So now I made sure I was the one doing the leaving, and that suited me just fine.

I arrived home, kicked off my shoes, and got cozy on my couch to devour my late-night snack. As I was eating, my thoughts drifted back to my romp in the hay with good old what's-his-name. He was okay, but not a worthy contender for a repeat. You'd have to really fuck like a god to get that kind of invitation. Believe me, I knew it was easier to recycle a good lay, but lately they'd been hard to come by. The last guy I deemed even remotely worthy of a repeat went and found himself a girlfriend, unfortunately. So I was back to picking up randos at the bar after work. If I were smart, I'd swear off men altogether and get myself off, but I've never been one to make the smartest decisions, and I was apparently a glutton for punishment.

2

———————

BRANDON

With my head bent over my sketchbook, I tuned out the rest of the shop. I still had some time before my next appointment, and I really wanted to finish this sketch. I hadn't had inspiration like this in years, so I had really been leaning into it lately. My last muse was my ex, Miranda. At one point in our relationship, I thought she was my endgame, but when things got tough, she checked out. At the lowest point in my life, the person who was supposed to be there by my side through it all disappeared. Truthfully, I probably would have left myself too, because after my mom died, I was a mess.

But looking back, Miranda was done with me months before my mom actually passed away. She hated how much time I spent at the hospital with my mom or helping around my parents' house. Not exactly how I'd want my life partner to act while my mom was dying, but I ignored her red flags because I didn't want to go through losing my mom alone.

Sure, I had my dad and my brothers, but they were dealing with their own grief.

Then, when Mom died, I completely broke. I didn't handle things well at all and fell into a pretty deep depression. I checked out of life because what was the point? At least, that's what I thought back then. A couple of months after my mom passed away—a questionably respectable amount of time to wait before dumping your boyfriend—Miranda left. Even though she was already gone emotionally, she ghosted me with no explanation.

So, there I was, depressed and grieving, and the girl I once thought I'd spend my life with abandoned me, too. I was glad I dodged that bullet, but at the time, it was just another thing that pushed me further into depression. I stopped living my life, rarely leaving my apartment. Bathing was a chore, and at that point, I'd lost so much weight, you'd think I was the one who had gone through cancer treatments. Thankfully, even though they were grieving too, my dad and brothers rallied and helped me see how badly I was handling everything. I was at my rock bottom, and after spending a week at an inpatient facility, I followed up with an outpatient therapist each week. Embarrassed as I was, I was also thankful that I got the help I needed—it saved my life.

Although it had been years, and I was back to my easy going self, now and then, I'd feel the sting of that abandonment. It's something I was sure I'd carry for the rest of my life, but now have coping mechanisms in place to deal with those feelings when they come up.

The bell above the front door signaled someone entering the shop, pulling me out of my thoughts. I looked up to see my brother, Nathan, walk in, followed by his new girlfriend, Daphne. Lowering my eyes, I continued with my sketch. I'd say hi to them in a minute. I really needed to get this sketch on paper while the idea was still fresh in my mind, and I still had a few minutes until my next appointment.

Moments later, I heard a throat clear, and I looked up to see the very subject of my sketch leaning up against my workspace. I quickly slapped my sketchbook closed.

Her arms crossed in front of her, pushing up her already ample chest. "Jumpy much?" She asked, leaning into my space. "Whatcha drawing?"

"What are you doing here?" I answered, avoiding her question as I pushed the book out of her reach and leaned back in my chair, trying to remain calm. She was the last person I expected to see.

"Daphne and I are getting bestie tattoos," Lexi beamed back at me. "Nathan made us appointments."

"Are you my one o'clock?" I asked hopefully. It had been about a month since that debacle of a Halloween party, and I hadn't been able to get her out of my mind since. When shit hit the fan, I didn't have time to say goodbye or get her number, so I was hoping we'd run into each other now that Nathan and Daphne had made things official.

"It's me or Daphne, and I guess Dylan is doing the other, although the tattoo we settled on is so tiny I don't know why we're taking up two of your appointment times." She pulled out a piece of paper from her purse to show me the design of two intertwined hand-drawn hearts.

"Did you draw these?" I asked.

"Yeah, we each drew one heart. I thought it was a cute idea and vanilla enough for Daphne's boring ass," she laughed.

"I can hear you, bitch," Daphne called from the front of the shop, causing Lexi and me to chuckle.

"I'd love to tattoo you, if that's okay?" I stood and started clearing my workspace.

"Yeah, that's fine with me," she smiled and then turned towards the front. "Daphs, Brando is going to do me." My cock twitched.

"He'd better do no such thing, Lexi. Behave yourself." Daphne joked back at her. God, did I want to do her alright, but I needed to keep my thoughts on the task at hand.

Lexi turned back to me. "Where do you want me?"

Her question had me imagining all the ways I'd like to have her—on my chair, bent over my desk, back at my place… the list went on and on. I shook my head. "Well, where do you want your tattoo?"

"I think right here, by my collarbone." She pointed to a spot over her left breast, and I think I stopped breathing. Tattooing had never been a sexual thing for me before. It didn't matter where the tattoo placement was; it was art on a canvas to me. But the thought of touching Lexi anywhere had me half hard already. I really needed to focus.

I turned away from her to adjust myself and get some supplies from a cabinet. I got to work setting up my station and motioned to the chair when it was ready. "You can sit here." She hopped up into my chair, and I began her consultation. We chatted about size and placement, and then I went into the back room to make the stencil. When I returned, I had her stand up so she could see the placement in a full-length mirror. After confirming everything looked good, I had her get back up on the chair. The tattoo was literally going to take me less than ten minutes, so I took my time getting started. I wanted to spend as much time as I could getting to know her.

"So, you mentioned this was pretty vanilla? If you could get any tattoo, what would it be?" I asked, curious about her.

She bit her lip, deep in thought, and damn if that wasn't sexy as hell. "I don't even like the ocean, but I love octopi. Or are they octopuses? Whatever. I love them. I think they are so beautiful and resilient, and they can adapt to so many situations, so I think I'd probably get an octopus or some tentacles or something."

"Octopi are cool. If you want, I can sketch up some ideas for you," I offered. "I think an octopus would look sick wrapped around your thigh."

"Oh, yeah? You checking out these meaty thighs?" She smacked, then grabbed onto one of her thick thighs and gave it a shake. I had to snap my mouth shut to keep from drooling.

I avoided her eyes. "How could I not?" *Was it getting hot in here?* My cheeks flamed. While I wasn't a player like Dylan, I also wasn't shy, and I definitely didn't blush when talking to a woman. Lexi affected me in ways I hadn't experienced before, but I needed to focus and not fuck up her easy-ass tattoo. "Now lean back and try to stay still. This won't take long at all."

"Ha! That's what he said," she laughed. "Well, I hope not, but you get the joke."

I grinned. "Yeah, I got it."

She leaned back, and I started her, checking in with her periodically to make sure she was okay. It was a small tattoo, just some fine lines, but it was still her first, so I wanted to make sure it was a pleasant experience for her.

I was leaning over her, finishing up, when she reached out and touched my arm. "Are you okay?" I asked, concerned that something was wrong.

"Yeah, I'm fine. I barely feel anything. I was just wondering what this tattoo says." She pointed to my forearm. From the angle of my arm, she couldn't quite make it out. I leaned back and shifted my arm so she could read it. With an arched brow, she asked, "Nice? Is there a story that goes along with it?" I lifted my other arm, and realization crossed her face. "Oh shit, you dirty bird."

I snorted. Yeah, my forearm tattoos were sort of a running joke in my family. One read *Naughty* and the other *Nice*. My little nod to my love of Christmas, but also to the two sides of me. Sure, I was a '*nice guy*,' but I also had a bit of a naughty side, especially in the bedroom. My brothers didn't know the specifics, but that didn't stop them from giving me shit about it. "What can I say? I love Christmas." I chuckled and got back to her tattoo.

"Mmhmm." She was too smart to believe that was the whole story, but didn't press the issue. Her eyes closed as she leaned back against the chair.

"All done," I said once the tattoo was complete. Lexi's eyes popped open as I was cleaning the area one last time so she could check it out. "Whatcha think?" I motioned for her to go to the mirror.

She jumped up and practically bounced to the mirror. "Oh, my God! I love it! Daphne, let me see yours!" Daphne had finished too and came back so they could compare and snap a selfie.

Dylan interrupted them so he could get a picture for our social media. He was good like that, and I appreciated it. I sucked at social media, and while I always took pictures for my portfolio, I was terrible about posting them.

"I still gotta cover that," I called after them. Lexi turned and gave me a huge grin. "Yes, sir," she saluted me. *Oop, that did it*. My dick twitched again.

As the girls chatted and took more pictures, I started cleaning, then Lexi came back to my station. "I just need a quick photo and then I'll cover it for you." I coaxed her back to the chair with my hand on the small of her back. A slight gesture that should have been nothing but felt too intimate. I wanted to touch her everywhere, but hurried my hand away.

After Lexi was back in my chair, I snapped a quick picture, covered her new tattoo, and went over aftercare instructions. Once I had gone over everything, I grabbed one of my cards from my desk and wrote my cell number on it. "If you have questions or need anything at all, don't hesitate to call. I put my cell on the back."

"Oh, did you now?" She gave me a wink. *Was she into me, too?* I probably should have asked for her number, but I was too much of a chickenshit. She made me nervous, and I didn't want to make things weird if she wasn't interested.

I cleared my throat. "Ahh, yeah." I pulled at the back of my neck. "Oh, and you can let me know about that octopus tattoo. If you decide you want me to sketch something up, shoot me a text."

"Yeah, that sounds good. Thanks. I'll let you know." Lexi hopped down from the chair, and we walked to the front. "How much do I owe you?" She asked as we reached the desk.

"It's on us," Dylan interrupted as I was about to say the same.

"No way. This is your business; we can't not pay," Daphne said as she and Lexi both started digging into their bags.

I put my hand on Lexi's arm. "Nope. Your money's no good here. Besides, these were small and didn't take up a lot of time. It's really no problem at all."

Lexi smiled up at me and laughed. "Thank you. That's really nice. I guess I'll get you next time for the octopus."

Daphne turned and wrinkled her nose. "What octopus?"

"My next tattoo! Now that Brando popped my cherry, I'm so ready for more," Lexi said excitedly and turned back to me. "Thanks again. I really love it. I'll let you know when I'm ready for my next one." Then she darted up on her toes and hugged me. I was so surprised that I barely had time to return her embrace before she was gone. The bell to the front door rang, and I vaguely recall Nathan and Daphne saying their goodbyes as I stood there replaying my whole interaction with Lexi.

"Fuck," Dylan said, drawing my attention back to the present. "Not you too."

3

———

LEXI

This Santa Claus is creeping me the fuck out, I thought as I made my way through the cafeteria to get myself a mid-shift snacky snack. In the far corner, there was a cute, makeshift North Pole so kids could visit with Santa. They had this set up every December, and I think they even had Santas making rounds on the pediatric floors so that the sick kids could tell Santa what they wanted for Christmas. I mean, aside from getting the hell out of here and getting better.

But this particular Santa was eyeballing me hard. *What the hell did I ever do to you, buddy? Whatever*. I moved through the cafeteria, grabbing some chips and a soda to take back up to the ICU break room. I had finished paying when I noticed Daphne chatting up Mister Creeper Claus. Okay, now I was interested.

"Hey bestie, whatcha doing?" I asked when I got close to them.

"Oh, hey Lex, you remember Brandon, right?" Daphne motioned towards Santa Claus.

I squinted my eyes, and I gave Santa another once-over. Yeah, I could see it now, and I could just barely see a tattoo peeking out from his collar. Brandon was gorgeous and would look good wearing a trash bag. He stood tall, maybe around six-foot-four, and built like a brick shithouse; I knew that under that fake beard and wig, he sported just the right amount of facial hair and wavy hair that he had worn in a loose man bun the couple of times I had seen him. He reminded me of a Norse god, but with darker features. As hot as he was in regular clothes, this getup definitely had me hot for Santa. My face must have given my thoughts away because Daphne hit me in the arm. "Ew, stop it."

"What? I didn't do anything," I shot back.

Daphne rolled her eyes.

I ignored her. "Hey, Brando, nice getup," I said with a wink.

"Thanks, um, you too. Um, I like your scrubs." Brandon's cheeks flamed. *Shit, was he flustered?*

I laughed and put a hand on my hip. "Yeah, I know, right? I look sooooo hot, I'm sure." I knew I looked a mess, with my dark hair piled on top of my head, not a stitch of makeup on, and there were most definitely bodily fluids splattered on my leg.

Brandon smiled and interrupted my self-deprecating thoughts. "Yeah, you look great, actually."

Daphne was looking between us with wide eyes, then

shook her head. "I gotta get back to the unit. See ya Sunday, Brandon."

"I'm coming too." I turned to follow her. "See ya, Brando." I waved back at him.

"Bye, Lexi." He smiled and then turned his attention towards a boy who had walked up to see Santa.

I caught up with Daphne by the elevators. "What's happening on Sunday?"

She turned to face me as we waited for the elevator. "We're having dinner at his dad's place."

"Oooo, I like dinner. Got room for one more?" I asked, trying to be as nonchalant as possible. I was interested in Brandon. He was fucking gorgeous and looked like he could break me in half, and I was eager to let him try. Was I interested in more than sex? Nope, but I needed an in.

Daphne leaned in and whispered, "You cannot fuck him. Do you hear me?"

"What the hell?" I hissed. "I wasn't planning on it," *Lie.* "but wanna tell me why exactly?"

"Um, because he's Nathan's brother, and not even the fuckboy brother. Dylan, I'd probably let you have a whack at, but please, not Brandon. He's too nice. I don't think he'd survive you." Daphne insisted as we entered the elevator.

"Dramatic much? Jeez, Daphne, you act like I'm some kind of man-eating succubus," I huffed and crossed my arms.

"I'm saying exactly that, babe. I love you, but you, my friend, are a fuckgirl, and Brandon is a good guy. You literally have the pick of the litter in this city, and I've seen you bag any guy you set your sights on. I don't want things to be weird at family dinners when you break Brandon's heart." Daphne was definitely overreacting.

"Break his heart? Who said anything about feelings?" I rolled my eyes. "I'm not trying to date anyone."

"Exactly. Promise me you'll leave Brandon alone. He's not looking for casual," Daphne pleaded as we exited the elevator.

"Fine. I promise not to bang your boyfriend's brother, jeez," I begrudgingly agreed. How was she going to tell me who I can and can't fuck? My bestie was being awfully judgey.

Truthfully, I wasn't even mad that she didn't want me to get involved with Brandon. She was right, after all—I *was* a fuckgirl, and I had no intention of changing my ways any time soon. Plus, if Brandon was as sensitive as she implied, then I shouldn't risk him getting attached, especially if Daphne and his brother were getting serious. But that didn't stop me from daydreaming about riding him while he wore that Santa suit. *New kink unlocked.*

THE REST of our shift was peacefully uneventful. Working in the ICU could be crazy, and I was always thankful for the slower, less hectic days. That day in particular was actually so slow that Daphne got to go home early. Of course, she'd be spending the night at Nathan's, leaving me free. *Again.* I was happy for her, truly, but it had been nice having her all to myself for those few weeks after she and fuckface broke up. Since then, I was keenly aware of how alone I was. I didn't have many friends because I kept most people at arm's length, so when I met Daphne, it surprised me how quickly I let her in. We became fast friends, and I clung to her like a lifeline. But now that she was blissfully in love, I had to keep myself occupied with other extracurricular activities.

Speaking of which, *where did that sexy-ass Santa go?* I thought as I passed the cafeteria on my way out of the hospital. To my dismay, the North Pole was closed, and he was nowhere in sight. *Bummer.* I still had an itch that needed scratching, so I guessed I was going out for the night.

I quickly made my way home and reheated some leftovers for dinner. I decided I'd go to my local watering hole rather than a club. Clubs could be fun, but I felt more comfortable in jeans and a cute top rather than having to get all dolled up in my sluttiest attire to go to the club. It was usually too much effort for only mediocre rewards. Guys at the clubs were usually looking to score, but they were almost too easy and usually only out to please themselves in bed. *I'm making generalizations, of course, and from time to time, I'd been pleasantly surprised.* But statistically, going to my local dive bar was easier and more fruitful. I could dress how I wanted and relax at the bar with a drink, and if the fish weren't biting, I wasn't out too much time or effort.

Daphne was right, though. I usually got any guy I went

after. Although I didn't think I was what most men were looking for. I wasn't rail-thin with huge tits. I was taller than most and a little thicker in the middle. Sure, I had a cute face and a nice rack, and my ass was probably the envy of a lot of women, but I didn't think I was what you'd call *traditionally* beautiful. Don't get me wrong, I loved every inch of my voluptuous body, but growing up seeing supermodels on TV and in ads, I knew what some people thought when they saw me. That didn't stop me from getting mine. I think it was my confidence that initially drew men in, and once I had them interested, it was all over.

The Basement was busy for a Thursday, but I managed to find a seat at the end of the bar. As the name implied, The Basement was in the basement of a building around the corner from my place. It was a dank dive bar, and I absolutely loved it. One of my favorite bartenders, Diane, was working, and she gave me a nod. She already knew what I wanted to drink. I was predictable that way. As she set my vodka soda with extra limes down in front of me, I thanked her and scanned the bar. There were a few couples canoodling and a group of girls laughing, huddled together. By the pool tables were a few guys, but not anyone who caught my attention. Unfortunately, I was still thinking about Brandon, and no one here was stacking up to that hunk of a man.

I sipped my drink, lost in thought, when a guy approached me. "Is this seat taken?" he asked. *Real original, buddy*, I thought.

"It's all yours," I answered without looking up. I heard

the scrape of the chair against the floor and finally looked up to see fucking Brandon sitting down next to me. *What the fuck?* "What are you doing here?" I asked, turning to face him.

"Nice to see you again, too, Lexi," he chuckled. "I was dropping something off at Nathan's, and this is on the way home. Just came to grab a beer."

"No fucking way you randomly ended up at *my* bar?" There was no fucking way.

"It's almost as if fate led me here," he said with a straight face. *Was this motherfucker for real right now?*

"Don't start that shit again, Brando." Diane set a beer down in front of him, and I must have looked as shocked as I felt, causing Brandon to let out a laugh.

"Start you a tab, Brandon?" Diane asked. "Or just the one tonight?"

My jaw hung open, my eyes wide. There was no fucking way that he'd been coming here, and we never ran into each other. *How was that even possible?*

"Seeing as how my good friend Lexi is here, you can start me a tab," he answered, and then turned to face me fully. "So, I guess you come here often?"

4

BRANDON

The look on her face was priceless. "So this is *your* bar?" I asked, amused as shit at how frazzled she seemed.

She ignored my jab. "How do you know Diane? If you were a regular, I'd have seen you before today."

I laughed. "Don't worry, Sweetheart, I'm not stalking you or anything. Diane is a client of mine, and so is her boyfriend. I've been here a few times."

"Ew, don't you Sweetheart me. It seems suss that you would show up here of all places."

"Or kismet," I half-joked. "You know, like how Daphne and Nathan met."

She squinted her eyes at me. "I can't tell if you're being for real right now or if you're just fucking with me. I hope, for your sake, it's the latter."

"You'd rather me be fucking with you?" I asked, amusement in my tone.

She scoffed, "Yeah, remember, I don't believe in that fate crap. I also don't do relationships, so if you thought this was your *in*, you're barking up the wrong tree, my guy."

"Don't worry, Sweetheart, I'm fucking with you," *I lied*. "Don't get your panties in a knot." Coincidence or fate, it didn't matter to me. I was just happy to see her again. The truth of the matter was, I had been thinking a lot about her since we first met at that Halloween party. Then, when I tattooed her last month, I knew I needed to see her again. Today, when I saw her in her scrubs at the hospital, all I could think of was getting her out of them and making her scream my name. Running into her yet again here at the bar had me convinced there had to be a reason.

"My panties are most certainly not in a knot." She rolled her eyes. "Anyway, shouldn't you be off getting toys ready for Christmas or something?" She sounded annoyed, but looked amused.

"Still thinking about me in that Santa suit, huh?" I teased.

"You wish," she groaned.

"Okay, okay, I'm done messing with you. How's your tattoo doing? You didn't text, so I'm assuming it's healing alright?"

She pulled the collar of her shirt down and strained to look at her collarbone. "I don't know. You tell me," she said as she thrust her chest towards me. *Good Lord.*

"Mmm, looks good to me. Have you given any more thought to your next one?" I asked, hopeful that I'd get her in my chair again.

"Not really, but I definitely like that octopus idea. I think that would be cool," she said and flipped her hair over her shoulder. "Why don't you draw me something so I can visualize it better?"

Turning to face her, I said, "I'd love to. I'll work on something this week and text you. Guess that means I need your number?"

"I guess so," she said coyly. "Here, give me your phone. I'll put my number in." I handed my phone to her, and she quickly typed in her info before handing it back to me. "Can't wait to see what you come up with."

"I should have something for you by next week." Noticing her drink was empty, I asked, "Can I get you another drink?"

She thought about it for a moment and then agreed, "Okay, one more." She pushed her glass out in front of her, and I motioned to Diane for another. Lexi turned to face me completely. "So, you gonna tell me the story behind these?" She leaned closer and drew her finger across my forearm, over my '*naughty*' tattoo. She was making pretty intense eye contact and leaning in close. If I didn't know better, I'd think she was flirting with me.

"Well, I love Christmas. It's actually my favorite holiday and one of the reasons I play Santa at the hospital each year." There were other reasons, but I wasn't trying to kill the vibe. "But as for these," I gestured to my arms. "I'm clearly no stranger to body art, and I wanted to add something to represent my love of Christmas, but also the two sides of my personality. People mostly see the nice guy side, but there's more to me than meets the eye," I winked at her, suddenly feeling bolder. The shyness I had felt during our earlier meetings faded away.

"Oh, yeah? So you have a naughty side, then?" She purred and moved her hand to my thigh. My cock twitched, and I let out a slight groan.

"Lexi," her name a whisper on my lips, and then Diane came with another round of drinks. "Thanks," I murmured as I moved away from Lexi slightly to sip my beer.

Lexi backed away and took a long sip of her drink, looking a little flushed. She set her drink back on the bar and turned to face me again, wiping her hands over her thighs. She bit her lip and then looked up into my eyes. "Listen, I'm going to say something right now, and if I'm totally out of line, let me know, okay?"

I eyed her suspiciously. "Okay?"

"Daphne told me I can't fuck you, but I want to." She exhaled a long breath. "I really fucking want to."

I stood quickly, probably catching her off guard, and raised my hand towards Diane at the other end of the bar. "Close me out."

AFTER QUICKLY SETTLING OUR TAB, I practically dragged Lexi out of the bar and stuffed her into my car. Okay, maybe that's an exaggeration, but I was moving quickly. I didn't want her to overthink things and change her mind. Or maybe it was me who didn't want to overthink things. Sleeping with Lexi could get messy, but at that moment, I didn't give a shit.

We didn't talk much on the way to my place, and thankfully, it was only a few minutes away. Once we got there, I parked, and we walked to my apartment in silence. I hoped she wasn't second-guessing her decision. "You okay?" I asked as we got to the door of my building.

She looked up at me and licked her lips. "Yep," she answered, popping the P. Tracing a finger down my chest, she continued, "When I'm finished with you, you won't even know your own name." *Oh shit!*

I turned and made quick work of the lock and ushered her inside. My apartment was one flight up, and we rushed up the steps. I fumbled slightly with my keys before finally opening the door to my apartment. Once inside, I slammed the door and turned to push her against it, but she was quicker than me. I looked down, and she was already on her knees, her deft fingers starting to undo my jeans.

"Whoa," I placed my hands over hers. "What are you doing?" I wasn't used to a woman taking control like that, not that I was complaining, but she caught me off guard.

"I'm going to see what we're working with here," she smiled wickedly, looking up at me through her dark eyelashes. "See if you're worth my time."

"Worth your time? I'll show you worth your time." And with that, I scooped her up and threw her over my shoulder, giving her plump ass a playful smack.

Lexi let out a surprised scream and then started cackling, "Bring it, Brando!" *This fucking woman.* I smacked her ass again. *Hard.* She yelped but didn't protest, and as I threw her down onto my bed, she looked up at me with fire in her crystal blue eyes.

I pulled my shirt up over my head and flung it to the side. I undid the buttons of my jeans, and Lexi's gaze followed my every move. Right as I was about to let my cock spring free, I stopped. Lexi licked her lips and stared up at me, cocking her head to the side inquisitively. "Show me what *you're* working with, Sweetheart," I taunted. "I wanna make sure you're worth *my* time." Lexi scoffed and rolled her eyes dramatically. Whatever she was going to say, I interrupted her. "Don't be a brat, Lexi, or I'll have to punish you."

"Like I said, bring it." Then she stuck out her tongue at me.

I reached down and dragged her to the edge of the bed by her ankles. "What a smart mouth you have. Let's see what else it can do." I opened my jeans the rest of the way, and my erection broke free immediately, causing Lexi's eyes to practically bulge out of her head. I knew what I was working with. My cock wasn't small by anyone's standards, and clearly she liked what she saw.

She wasted no time getting to her knees. "Yes, sir," she said as she licked her lips again. "Damn, Brandon. I guess you are gonna be worth it. I just hope you aren't a two-pump chump."

I laughed and shook my head. "Jesus, Lexi." I stopped laughing pretty quickly though, because the next thing I knew, she had one hand on my thigh, the other cupping my balls, and her tongue was licking my shaft from base to tip. "Oh, God." I groaned.

She backed away slightly and said with a wink, "That's Goddess to you," and then took me to the back of her throat. My knees almost buckled as she continued to suck and lick me with just the right amount of pressure. *Damn, this girl knew how to suck a dick,* and that thought gave me a second of pause before I thought, *fuck it,* and started fucking her throat. She hummed around my cock, drawing me closer to the edge. I was close. *Too close.*

I pulled her off of me and pushed her back onto the bed. Her face was flushed, her eyes glassy, and her mascara trailed down her cheeks. She looked up at me questioningly, but before she could voice her question, I said, "My turn, Sweetheart. Strip." And she did. As I slowly stroked my cock, she quickly removed her jeans and pulled her shirt up over her head. She sat there before me in her lacy black bra and thong. She looked every bit the goddess she claimed to be, her curves on full display. I crossed my arms over my chest and jerked my chin. "All of it."

"Jeez, so pushy," she teased. But teasing Brandon was gone. Seeing her like this unraveled me. I was a feral beast with one goal—*to please this woman.* My eyes were laser-focused on her as she peeled off her bra and slipped out of her thong. Her eyes met mine, and there was no shyness in them, only desire and need.

I leaned down and grabbed her ankles, dragging her to

the edge of the bed slowly. "Now, show me how wet you are for me, Lexi."

She bent her knees and placed her feet flat on the bed before spreading her legs to reveal the effect I was having on her. Her pussy glistened in the low light. She looked me right in the eyes as she swiped two fingers through her center and then brought them to her mouth, licking them seductively. I gripped my unbearably hard cock in my hand again and stroked it forcefully.

"Tsk, tsk. Now, who's the naughty one?" I wagged my finger at her. "Who said you could have a taste of what's mine?"

Her fingers found her center again, and she started toying with her clit. "Better come and take it then before I finish," she moaned.

I kneeled and pressed my hands against her thighs to give me more room. The scent of her arousal was sharp and intoxicating, making my mouth water with need. She was still strumming her clit, so I swatted her hand away.

Her protests were cut short when I licked through her center slowly, stopping on her sensitive clit to suck on it slightly, earning me a heady moan. "Ohhhh, fuuucccckkk." I continued to lap at her wetness, taking everything she was offering until she was a squirming, pleading mess. "Please, Brandon. More."

I sat back and raised an eyebrow. "Oh, so it's Brandon now? No more smart mouth?"

"Shut the fuck up and do that again." I snickered but complied, diving back in to feast on her. This time, adding one thick finger inside of her tight pussy, causing her to grip the hair on my head tightly. "You like that, Sweetheart?" I asked while adding a second finger and curling them inside of her.

"Yes!" she cried out. "Yes, Brandon, that feels so good."

While pumping my fingers in and out of her, I sucked on her clit until I could feel her clenching around them like a vise. I couldn't wait to feel her come like this on my dick. I continued to fuck her with my fingers through her orgasm until she relaxed slightly. She looked totally blissed out, and I wanted to give her time to recover, but I also couldn't wait to be inside her.

I sat back and took her in. She was smiling, with a dazed look in her eyes. "Are you okay?" I asked. I knew she was okay, but I was trying to gauge if she truly needed a minute or not.

Then she looked me dead-ass in the eyes and said, "Brando, you just finger-banged me into oblivion. I am fan-fucking-tastic." She smiled and flopped her head back on the bed.

"Oh, my Goddess. You are fucking wild," I chuckled. "But I'm not finished with you yet." I crawled up her body, nipping, licking, and kissing my way to her breasts, where I stopped to worship them. "Look at these fucking tits, Lex. Fuucckk." I took a stiff nipple into my mouth as I caressed the other. She arched her back and pushed her chest up into my touch.

"Brandon, I want you to fuck me," she begged. "Please."

I moved the rest of the way up her body, touching her everywhere, leaving a trail of wet kisses in my wake. When I reached her face, I paused to stare into her eyes before capturing her lips with mine. Her breathing hitched, and she froze for a moment before finally melting into me. Our kiss stretched on, our tongues frantically exploring. I was painfully hard and ground my cock into her pelvis to find some relief.

She broke our kiss. "Fuck. Me. Now," she rasped out.

I jumped up to grab a condom from the nightstand. With my teeth, I hastily tore the wrapper and sheathed myself while staring into Lexi's eyes, her breath catching at the promise of what was to come. I quickly positioned myself over her again before *oh-so-slowly* pushing inside of her with a groan. Her body tensed, and she held her breath as her body attempted to accommodate my girth. "Breathe," I whispered as I paused my movement.

She reached behind me and grabbed my ass to pull me in further. "Just fuck me."

I started moving again. Slowly at first, but she was meeting my slow thrusts, encouraging me to move faster. I picked up the pace and was rewarded with the sounds of Lexi's enthusiastic moans. "Yes, Brandon, yes. Harder."

She asked, and I delivered, thrusting harder and faster. I captured her mouth with mine again, my hand pinching one of her taut nipples. She moaned into my mouth. Falling into a steady rhythm, I could feel her pussy squeezing me with every thrust. I braced one arm by her head and reached down with my other hand and began circling her clit with my thumb. She moaned her approval and then, moments later, came hard around me, pushing me over the edge to find my own release.

"This can never happen again," she breathed as I collapsed onto her.

"We'll see about that," I chuckled into her neck.

5

LEXI

"No, I'm serious. Daphne is going to kill me," I sighed as I tried to push Brandon off of me.

"Whoa, what's the hurry?" he protested.

"This was a mistake. I gotta go." I pushed him again, and that time he rolled over to the side enough that I could get up.

As I was getting off the bed, he grabbed my wrist. "Wait a minute, please. Don't run off," he pleaded.

Ripping my arm out of his grasp, I started gathering my discarded clothes from where they lay strewn across the room. "I can't. I'm serious, Brandon. That was great, really, but it cannot happen again because I promised Daphne I wouldn't." I continued to spiral. "I can't believe I did that. She's going to kill me. Forget this happened."

"No chance of that, Sweetheart," he answered with a grin that made my clit pulse. He sat back against the headboard and put his hands up behind his head. He didn't even have the decency to cover himself, so that monster between his legs was staring back at me, too.

"And stop calling me Sweetheart!" I practically shouted as I haphazardly threw my clothes on. I needed to get the fuck out of there. If I didn't, there was a good chance that I'd jump on top of him and go for round two. I looked away and dug my phone out of my purse. I needed an Uber, stat.

"Okay, Lexi. Can you sit down for a second?" Brandon was being so calm and reasonable, but everything in me was telling me I needed to run for the hills. His infuriatingly handsome smile, his charming personality, *that monster hog* —he was too good to be true. Regardless, I wasn't interested.

"No thanks. I'm calling an Uber." I held up my phone and looked back in his direction. That was a mistake because he was hard again and stroking that beast of a cock with a devilish look in his eye.

"Are you sure I can't tempt you to stay?" he said and then licked his lips slowly.

"Are you fucking kidding me?" I screeched. "I thought you were the nice brother."

"Like I said, sometimes I can be naughty, too." Then that motherfucker actually winked at me.

I moved closer to the bed, my legs moving of their own volition. Brandon lifted his chin. "Come on, Sweetheart, come sit on Santa's lap."

I squeezed my thighs together, tension already building back between them. I closed my eyes and took a deep breath. He knew exactly what he was doing, and it was working. He was the kind of fuck that I'd want a repeat of, again and again. I knew better than to give in, but my pussy had a mind of her own sometimes. Like at that moment, that treacherous bitch was calling the shots. "Fuck it," I breathed as my eyes popped open. I mean, I'd already fucked him once. A second round wouldn't change anything.

Brandon's smile cracked wide across his face. "Fuck, yeah. Get that sexy ass back in this bed." He stopped stroking himself long enough to grab a fresh condom and sheath himself.

I tossed my phone and purse back onto the floor and made quick work of removing my clothes again. Then I crawled onto the bed and straddled him. Using the headboard for support, I hovered above him and took his cock in my hand, giving it a rough tug. A deep growl erupted from his chest. I gave him one more squeeze before lifting up and impaling myself on him. *Oh, fuck yes!* His cock was perfection, and coming from a cock connoisseur like me, that was saying something.

He grabbed onto my hips, squeezing and massaging my flesh, guiding my movements as I rode him. I arched my back, and his mouth found my breast, licking and sucking on my stiff nipple. I leaned into him more, angling myself so that my clit rubbed his pelvic bone. Working in short rhythmic thrusts, I brought us both to the edge again quickly. He started thrusting up into me more forcefully, and I cried out as my orgasm enveloped me. I kept up my pace through my climax and then grabbed Brandon's face between my hands. Looking him in the eyes, I asked, "So, Santa, what's the verdict? Am I on the naughty or nice list?"

A deep laugh escaped him, and suddenly I was being tossed from his lap, and he was behind me, pushing back into me. From this angle, I could feel his size more acutely. *Damn, he was big.*

"You've been a naughty girl, Sweetheart." He gripped my hips hard and pounded into me. "Ready for your punishment?"

"Do your worst," I taunted.

"You're such a brat, Lexi." *Whack!* His hand came down hard on my ass, but his other hand held firm at my hip, holding me in place.

"Again," I encouraged him. I loved a little pain with my pleasure, and most of my one-night stands were too chickenshit to give me what I craved most. His hand came down again, and I pushed back into him. "More."

"You like it when it hurts, don't you, baby?"

"Mmmhmm," I hummed in response.

He gripped my hair at the back of my head and pulled me up so my back was to his chest, but kept up his pace, driving into me deeper somehow at the new angle. One hand wrapped around my throat, and the other moved to toy with my swollen clit. I reached up to squeeze his hand on my throat. Hopefully, he recognized that this was me giving consent for more and not telling him to stop. Understanding what I wanted, his grip on my throat tightened, and I could feel that euphoria creeping closer. *Just a little more.* Black spots dotted my eyes. His fingers circled my clit at a steady speed and pressure while his cock continued to fill me.

"Come for me, Lexi," he breathed into my ear. And then, right when I thought I might pass out, stars danced behind my closed eyes, and that euphoria I was so desperate for spread throughout my body. I came hard as Brandon released his grip on my neck and moved his arm to my waist to steady me. "Good girl." His paced slowed as he fucked me through another orgasm, finding his own release a few moments later.

Exhausted, I fell onto the bed, unable to move or form words. I felt the bed shift as Brandon lifted me to right me in the bed, placing my head on a pillow. He crawled in behind me and covered us with a light blanket, wrapping his strong arm around me. This is usually when I'd be running for the fucking hills, and I would as soon as my body started working again. But I was so comfortable and so satisfied, I just lay there and let it happen.

I woke with my heart pounding as I took in my surroundings. I was still at Brandon's, his muscular arm still wrapped around me. His warm, woodsy scent invaded my senses. *How the fuck did I let this happen? What time was it?* It was still dark, at least, but I needed to get out of there.

Brandon's steady breathing told me he was asleep. The chances of my getting out of there without waking him were slim, but I attempted to move his arm so I could get up. He tightened his grip. "Mmmm, where do you think you're going?" he murmured at my neck.

Fuck. "I gotta pee," I lied. Well, I guess it wasn't a lie. I did actually have to pee, but more importantly, I needed a reason to get up and leave.

He gave me a squeeze, kissed the side of my head, and released me. "Hurry back," he whispered as he rolled over. *I don't fucking think so.*

Quietly gathering my things, I hurried into the en suite, thankful for the sliver of light peeking through the curtain from a street lamp. I shut the door softly and then flipped on the light. *Damn, I looked like a hot fucking mess.* Wild hair and mascara everywhere. I checked my phone. 2:11 am. *Yep, time to go.* I ordered an Uber and then threw on my clothes. Flicking the light off, I slowly opened the bathroom door and tiptoed out of Brandon's room. A floorboard in the hall creaked, and I froze.

"Lexi?" Brandon called groggily from his room.

Ignoring him, I kept going out the front door, down the stairs, and walked to the corner where my Uber would pick me up.

6

———

BRANDON

*F*uuuuccckk. The front door clicked shut, and I flopped back onto my pillow with a huff. *Damn, Lexi couldn't get out of here fast enough.* I knew she said Daphne would kill her for hooking up with me, but that couldn't really be why she bolted. I mean, they seemed pretty tight, and Daphne seemed like a reasonable person. If Lexi and I wanted to pursue something, I was sure she'd get over it. Lexi made it pretty clear she wasn't interested, but that was too fucking bad. Now that I had a taste, there was no way I was done with her.

THE NEXT MORNING, I woke up and started my day as usual, with a hot cup of coffee and my sketchbook. My dining room table overlooked a small park that was blanketed in a light dusting of snow. I loved sitting there in the mornings to sketch or plan my day. My morning routine also included staying unplugged until I had my coffee, a habit that I started a few years ago. Before that, I used to get on my phone first thing in the morning and would get so distracted by life that my mornings felt rushed and stressful. After starting this habit, I found my days started more peacefully. But right now, wondering if Lexi had texted me was disrupting my usual peaceful morning routine. I was sure she hadn't, but I couldn't stop thinking about her, so I grabbed my phone off its charger in the kitchen to check. *Nope. Of course, she didn't text.*

I typed out a message.

ME

Good morning.

There. Simple. Not weird. Just a normal message to say good morning. *Right? Should I say something about last night?* She left so quickly. *Maybe she was regretting it? Maybe she didn't have a good time? Not fucking possible.* I knew she enjoyed herself because I made sure of that. My mind raced with all the reasons she could have run out of here last night, and none of them calmed me. Maybe it was really because Daphne would be mad.

ME

I won't tell anyone, if that's what you're worried about.

ME

I had a great time, though, and I'd love to see you again.

Shit. I needed to stop now. I was spiraling. My phone dinged with an incoming message, and I braced myself for her response.

LEXI

Bro, it's 7 am. I'm asleep. Stop freaking out.

I chuckled. Yeah, I guessed it was a little early. Especially since we had a late night.

ME

Sorry… You left in a hurry last night, so I wanted to check in to make sure you were okay.

LEXI

I'm fine. The sex was great. We will NOT be doing that again, though. I'm going back to bed.

Well, fuck. She shot me down before I could even make my case. I'd have to work on that tattoo idea for her. That would give me a reason to message her again, and, hopefully, she'd still be open to letting me tattoo her again. I put my phone down and opened my sketchbook to the place where I had left off yesterday. Pale blue eyes stared back at me, and I quickly flipped the page to work on something else. Something that would get me back into Lexi's orbit.

By the time I put my pencil down, my coffee was cold,

and the morning was gone. I was so lost in my work; I hadn't noticed the time passing. I had a few afternoon appointments, so I packed up my sketchbook and got ready for the rest of my day.

In the shower, my thoughts drifted back to my night with Lexi. She was perfect. Her *'I don't give a fuck attitude'* really did it for me for some reason. My cock was hard again, thinking about her. The feel of her pussy gripping my cock, her on her knees before me, the taste of her. I groaned and gripped my hard-on firmly, stroking myself under the warm spray of the shower. I pictured her in the shower with me, on her knees again, sucking my cock. Moments later, I came hard against the shower wall with my eyes closed tightly, visions of Lexi consuming me.

I ARRIVED at the shop after one o'clock in the afternoon. My dad and Dylan were already there working on clients. I gave them each a quick wave and a hello before heading back to my station. My first appointment wasn't due in until two, so I had plenty of time to set up and work on a few things before they arrived.

I unpacked my bag, laying out my sketchbook and pencil case. I wanted to work on Lexi's tattoo a little more so I would have something to show her sooner rather than later.

"Whatcha working on?" My dad asked as he came up

and sat on my station. I hadn't even noticed his client had left.

"Oh, hey, Pops. Just something for a friend." I answered somewhat truthfully. I mean, Lexi could be a friend.

He eyed my work. "Looks good. Where's it going to go?" he asked as he leaned over to get a better look.

"I'm thinking it would look sick wrapped around her thigh." I motioned to my own thigh, so he'd get a visual of where I was thinking.

"Oh, it's for a *girl* friend," he said, exaggerating the *'girl'* part.

"Dad, I've tattooed hundreds of women. It's not a big deal." He was being nosey. *Too nosey.* It wasn't a secret that I offered to work on a tattoo for Lexi, but he didn't need the details either.

"But how many of those did you consider to be friends?" he asked. "Last I checked, you hadn't had any friends of the female variety in quite a while."

"Oh, give it a rest, old man, and quit busting my balls. It's not that big of a deal. Daphne's friend asked me to draw something up for her when they came in last month for their matching tattoos." I had nothing to hide, so I told him the truth. *There was no way he'd know it was more than that, right?*

"Mmmhmm. Okay, son. Whatever you say," he said with a wink and then hopped off my table to head back up front. *The fuck?*

I shook my head and packed up my supplies. My

appointment would be there soon, and I needed to stay focused on that.

7

———

LEXI

I couldn't stop thinking about him, and it started the moment I left his apartment. When I got home and crawled into bed after a hot shower, I felt sore in the best possible way. Then he texted me early the next morning, causing me to think of him again and the way he defiled me. He was a big guy, and even days later, I could feel the aftermath of his cock between my legs. Not that I was complaining—that's actually a massive compliment—but I knew I needed to stay away from him. Daphne made me promise not to fuck him, and what did my whore ass do? I fucked him at the first chance I got. Thankfully, he hadn't texted me again since that morning, so I didn't have to blow him off again. *Maybe he got the message after all?*

I spent the last few days relaxing and catching up on my favorite trash TV shows. I loved the drama of a good reality TV show—it was one of my guilty pleasures. But then I was back to my reality and back at work, unfortunately.

Being an ICU nurse was super rewarding, but it could also be super stressful. Today was one of those stressful days. I was assigned to be the code team nurse, and it must have been a full moon or some shit, because I'd been running to codes and rapid responses all damn morning.

At lunchtime, I clocked out and made my way to the cafeteria, thankful for the break. As I was walking in, I noticed Santa wasn't at his North Pole setup. *Why was I looking for him? It wasn't like I wanted to see him again, right?* Lost in thought, I was still looking toward the North Pole when I ran into what felt like a brick wall—a tall, velvety brick wall with a fake beard and red hat.

Brandon, aka Santa, grabbed me by my arms to steady me as I practically bounced off of him. "Hey, easy there. You okay?" he asked with a grin.

I stared up at him. *Fuck me, he looked good.* I felt so small in his arms, and that was such a turn on for me. I wasn't the smallest of girls, so I went absolutely feral for a guy who made me feel tiny.

"Lexi, are you okay?" he asked again, sounding more concerned. *Oops, I guess I hadn't responded.*

"Yeah, I'm fine," I said finally. "Come with me." I pulled him by the hand out of the cafeteria.

"What are you—" His words cut off as I pushed him into a vacant on-call room and locked the door behind us. "What are you doing, Lexi?"

A mischievous smile spread across my face as I stalked towards him. "I know I said it was a one-time thing, but I gotta tell you, this Santa suit just does something to me."

He held his hands up. "Whoa. Wait a minute. We can't do that here." His eyes darted around the room and to the door. He licked his lips and then clenched his fists. "Can we?" He was definitely game. I just needed to reassure him that we wouldn't get caught. People think this shit only happens on Grey's Anatomy, but I'm telling you, where there's a will, there's a way, and hospital workers have needs like anyone else.

"Don't worry, Santa. The door is locked, and I promise to be as quiet as a mouse." I moved closer and grasped his forearms tightly. "So what's it gonna be? Are you feeling naughty or nice today?"

Without a word, he gripped me firmly around the waist and lifted me, catching my mouth with his. My legs wrapped around him, and then he walked a few steps until my back slammed against the wall. I reached up and pulled off his stupid fake beard. As hot as the Santa shit was, it was also in the way. We continued to make out like a couple of horny teenagers, each of us licking and nipping at one another. His erection pressed against me, causing me to gasp.

"You see what you do to me, Sweetheart?" he growled.

"I need you inside of me. Now, Brandon," I pleaded. And then I remembered where we were and that I didn't have any goddamned condoms. *Fuck.*

His hands caressed and massaged my ass and thighs while he continued to dry hump me against the wall. Well, maybe *dry* hump wasn't the right term, because I was most definitely wet. I only hoped the evidence wouldn't be visible through my scrubs.

"Hmm, you want this cock, baby?" he asked breathlessly.

"Condom?" I asked, praying he was the prepared type and had one in his wallet or something. I couldn't believe I hadn't thought of it before, but Brandon had me all kinds of fucked up and totally off my game.

He pulled away to look me in the eyes. "I'm dressed as Santa, Lexi. Why would I have condoms with me?" he deadpanned.

"Fuck," I whined, more mad at myself than anything. "Let me down."

"Okay," he replied, but kept me in his grip and walked me over to the crummy twin bed in the corner of the room. He laid me down and then started untying my scrub pants, but I caught his hands with mine.

"We don't have condoms, Brando."

"That doesn't mean I can't get you off quick before you have to get back to work." I released his hands because, *fuck it*. If he wanted to get me off, who was I to say no?

He made swift work of my drawstring and pulled my pants and underwear down in one motion, leaving my shoes and socks on. *The fuck?* Suddenly, he pulled my legs up over his head and leaned in close, leaving my feet resting on his back. I hoped he dry-cleaned his suit regularly because these shoes had seen some shit, *literally*. Whatever, that was a later problem. Right now, I was more focused on the man in front of me, who was looking at my dripping pussy as if it were his last meal.

He started on my thigh, kissing and licking his way up, and then swiped his thick tongue through my center. He didn't waste any time, adding two fingers into my needy pussy while flicking and licking, and sucking on my clit. I was ready to blow in seconds. Then, I came hard, convulsing like I was being electrocuted. Fuck, I never came that fast with anyone else before. *Fucking clit whisperer.*

He eased up but kept slowly finger fucking me and sucking on my clit while I came down. "Fuck, Santa. That was so fucking hot."

He laughed from between my legs. "Yeah, it was. I could eat this pussy all day, every day." After putting my feet back down on the ground, he helped me stand so I could pull my pants up.

As I finished righting myself, the code pager went off. *Perfect timing.* I picked it up to show him. "Gotta run. Duty calls." I walked towards the door, but he grabbed me by the arm.

"Not so fast, Sweetheart. When can I see you again?" His devilish grin made him look more like a bad boy, not the nice guy Daphne had made him out to be.

"Maybe soon." I shrugged, offering him a glimmer of hope as I slipped out the door. Strangely enough, and against my better judgment, I did actually want to see him again. This guy could fuck, ate pussy like a pro, and, from what I could tell, I didn't hate his personality. As long as he could keep his mouth shut and feelings out of this, I wasn't opposed to keeping him in the rotation.

WHEN I GOT BACK to the unit from the fourth code of the day, I flopped down in a chair at the nurses' station. "Fuck today," I huffed quietly, so as not to be heard by any visitors.

Daphne and Amanda shot me a disapproving look. "Lexi," Daphne snapped. "Shhh."

I rolled my eyes. "First of all, don't shhh me. Second, I was whispering. No one heard me. And third, is it a fucking full moon? If I have to go to one more code today, I swear to God I'm quitting." I wasn't really going to quit, but I would threaten to at least once a week.

"You say that all the time," Amanda laughed. "And you keep coming back for more abuse."

"Whatever. So tell me what I missed. What's been happening here while I've been running all over the hospital saving lives?" Getting some juicy tea would help ease my annoyance at having to actually work. Don't get me wrong, I loved being a nurse and working in the ICU. Being the code nurse, though, was another story. In the ICU, I was pretty autonomous. We had a lot to do with patient care plans and their outcomes, but on the floors, during a code, we were under the direction of residents, some of whom didn't know their asses from their elbows and would fumble through a code looking at a freaking cheat sheet. It was quite annoying to be the smartest one in the room sometimes and not be able to take the lead. And let's just say that being diplomatic while correcting them was not necessarily my forte. I think my manager knew this and assigned me to the code team frequently so that I could improve. So far, it wasn't working.

Anyway, back to the tea... or lack thereof, apparently. "Nothing to report. Sorry to disappoint," Amanda chuckled.

"Yeah, it's been pretty quiet," Daphne said and then quickly slapped a hand over her mouth, her eyes wide.

"I cannot believe you just said that." Amanda looked at her as if she had kicked a kitten. It wasn't far off. Saying the 'Q' word in the hospital was a big no-no, and we all knew it. It was usually the kiss of death on a slow day.

"I swear to God, Daphne, if you just ruined my chances of getting out of here on time, I'm gonna kill you." I tacked on.

"It was an accident. I swear. I take it back," Daphne said as she got up out of her chair. "Welp, gotta go check on my patients."

"Okay. Text me later." I waved her off and then turned my attention to Amanda. "Hey, can you keep a secret?"

8

———

BRANDON

ucking Lexi. Every time I thought we were getting closer, she'd run. I wanted to know more about her, but how could I if the only time I got to spend with her was when we were fucking? Not that I was complaining about the fucking. That was top tier, but I wanted more.

I stayed in the on-call room for a few minutes after she had left. I needed time to get my raging hard-on under control and regain my composure. After all, I still needed to play Santa for the kids. I spent the rest of the day focused on them and trying my best not to think about Lexi.

After I left the hospital for the day, though, she consumed my thoughts, so I went home and finished up her tattoo sketch. Needing a reason to see her again that didn't involve sex, I sent off a text and attached the octopus I'd drawn for her tattoo.

ME

Hey, idk if you are still interested in that tattoo, but here's what I came up with. Let me know if you want to come by the shop to work out placement.

There, I kept it professional. Her reply came moments later.

LEXI

Wow, Brando. That looks great. Okay, I guess I could stop by this week. Let me know when.

LEXI

Also-today was hot AF, but if you tell anyone, I swear to God I will cut off that perfect cock of yours, have it stuffed, and use it without you.

I laughed so hard that I snorted.

ME

Perfect, huh?

LEXI

OMG, don't go getting a big head now.

ME

Apparently, it's too late for that, Sweetheart.

LEXI

Seriously, I know it shouldn't matter, but I made a promise and now I feel shitty about breaking that promise.

ME

Understood. Plus, I'd like to keep my dick
where it is, so I'll keep my mouth shut. I'll
look at my schedule and text you a few
options for when you can come in this
week.

LEXI

Okay, sounds good. Also, if you need me
to finish what I started earlier, I'm game.

I stared down at my phone in disbelief. Did she just
offer up a booty call?

ME

Sweetheart, are you saying you miss me
already?

LEXI

🙂 Why do you have to be so annoying?

ME

You say annoying. Some may say
charming.

LEXI

More like infuriating.

ME

Don't be a brat, Lexi, or I won't give you
what you want.

LEXI

Listen here, Brando, I've been doing fine
without you. I don't need you to get off.
I'm perfectly capable of finding someone
else to help me out.

ME

See what happens if you do. Try me.

LEXI

Bet.

This fucking woman was going to be the death of me.

9

LEXI

What a pompous ass. How dare he. I squeezed my thighs together to try to soothe the ache that was building there. Fuck, I wished he weren't so damn good-looking or so good at fucking. That would've made ignoring him so much easier, but no. He had to go and be the most devastatingly handsome man I'd ever seen and so amazing in bed that I couldn't stop thinking about him. *Rude.*

I'd show him I didn't need him to get off. I dressed quickly in my sluttiest top and a pair of snug-fitting jeans. After running a brush through my hair and swiping on a thick coat of mascara and lip gloss, I took in my reflection in the mirror. *Perfect.* Operation '*make Brando pay*' was in full swing.

I arrived at The Basement twenty minutes later, ready to find myself a cute guy to make Brando jealous. I knew I was being a brat, but I secretly hoped he'd come and punish me with a thousand orgasms. Step One of my plan was simple: Find a guy who was attractive enough and reel him in as I do. Step Two: Send a selfie to Brando so he knew where I was and who I was with. Step Three: Wait for him to show up and take me out of there. It was a win-win, really. Even if he didn't show, I'd fuck the other guy to get Brandon out of my system.

Being that it was a Friday night, the place was pretty busy, and there were plenty of options for me to choose from. I saddled up at the bar next to one option, and he immediately took the bait, turning towards me and offering to buy me a drink. *God, how was I so good at spotting the easy ones?*

Did I feel bad about using the guy? No, he was only buying me a drink, hoping to take me home and use me, so we were really using each other. We made small talk, and he asked me the typical surface-level-getting-to-know-you questions. Then, when I was good and bored with him, I slipped my phone out and shot off a text to Brandon, complete with a discreet selfie I had snagged that included enough of the bar that he'd know where I was and a bit of my new friend.

ME

Don't worry. I found someone to help me out.

I really was being a brat, but I didn't give one single solitary fuck. This was a game I was willing to play to get what I wanted, and at that moment, I wanted Brandon. I could see that he read my message, but no response came in.

He was either on his way or decided I wasn't worth his time. Turning towards my second choice, I smiled. If this guy ended up being my only option, I guessed I'd need to put in some sort of effort.

Fifteen minutes and another drink later, my chair slid roughly to the side, and Brandon now stood between me and option B. I smiled smugly up at him while option B got all huffy. "Hey, man. What's your deal?"

"Walk away," Brandon replied without even a glance in the guy's direction. Brandon's eyes shot daggers into mine. If looks could kill, I'd be dead.

"Listen, man…" option B started. Brandon closed his eyes and turned slowly, but before he could tell the guy to piss off, I pulled on his arm and leaned over so I could talk to option B.

"I'm good, my guy. Get lost."

Option B mumbled, not so under his breath, "Fucking bitch."

Oop! Brando did not like that. "What the fuck did you call her?" Brandon growled and leaned into his face.

Diane materialized before us. "Everything okay here?"

"Yep, we were just leaving. Right, Brando?" I pulled on his arm.

Brandon took a deep breath to calm himself and then turned towards me, his expression stony. A small screech escaped me as I was being hauled out of the bar over Brando's shoulder. *Fuck yes.*

10

BRANDON

When Lexi sent me that picture from The Basement, I laughed. I knew she was doing it to get me riled up, but when I got to the bar and saw her actually flirting with that guy, I saw red. There was not a chance in hell I was leaving there without her. As I made my way closer to where they sat at the bar, I noticed his hand on her back. *Nope. Not today and not ever.* She was *mine*. That thought should have scared the shit out of me, but it didn't. Even though we barely knew one another, I knew I wanted her to be mine.

The initial look of shock on her face as I pulled her chair away and stepped in between them was priceless. Relief washed over me as I realized she was actually happy I'd interrupted. The guy she'd been talking to ran his mouth, but I managed to keep my cool. The last thing I needed was to get arrested for teaching that smug asshole a lesson. I wanted to, believe me. Nothing would have given me more pleasure than to knock his ass out when I heard him call her a bitch. *Well, I can think of a few things that would give me more pleasure.* No one was ever going to talk to her like that again, at least not in my presence. As much as I wanted to hurt him, my priority was getting her out of that bar and back to my place. I had a punishment to dole out.

I carried her out of the bar over my shoulder as other patrons and employees either cheered or watched on quizzically. Diane shook her head as she went to help her next customer—probably just another night at The Basement for her. I was sure she'd seen worse and was just glad I didn't clobber the guy Lexi had been talking to.

I plopped Lexi into the passenger seat of my car without a word and then made my way to the driver's side. When I started the car, Lexi turned to face me, feigning indignation. "What the fuck, Brando? I was in the middle of something."

I raised an eyebrow and pinned her with a stare that told her I wasn't in the mood for her shit. She crossed her arms over her chest and faced forward again with a huff.

The drive to my place was quick and silent. My mind raced with all the things I wanted to do to her. I promised her a punishment, and I was more than ready to deliver. It was more than that, though. Lexi made me feel things I hadn't felt before—jealousy, possessiveness, this primal need to claim her, even though I knew she may never be mine in the way I wanted. Up until I saw her with that guy, I wasn't even sure that's what I wanted, but then I was. I wanted Lexi. All of her.

I parked and rounded the car, reaching her side as she

opened her door to get out. I picked her up and threw her back over my shoulder. Her protests fell on deaf ears as I made my way into the building and took the stairs two at a time. The entire room rattled as I kicked the door closed behind us after entering my apartment. I stormed into my bedroom and threw Lexi down on my bed.

At first, I was afraid that I was being too aggressive, and that she'd be frightened, but when I looked down at her, she had nothing but lust in her eyes. Pupils blown wide, her breathing was deep and ragged. She was as turned on as I was, but that was too damn bad. She wouldn't be coming anytime soon.

We stared at each other for a few moments before simultaneously starting to remove our clothes. We held eye contact as we stripped down to nothing. Lexi's smile stretched wide as I approached the bed slowly, with my painfully hard cock bobbing between us. Her eyes darted between my legs, and she licked her lips in anticipation.

"See something you like, Sweetheart?" I asked as I lowered myself onto the bed in front of her.

"Mmmhmm," she hummed.

I started crawling up her body. "You were being a brat earlier, Lexi. You know what that means?"

She rolled her eyes. "No, but I'm sure you're gonna tell me."

I kissed and licked my way up her body, avoiding all the places I was sure she wanted me most. "Good girls get orgasms, Lexi. Brats get punished," I breathed against her molten skin. She was so needy. This was going to be fun.

"Do your worst, Brando," she shot back. She probably thought she'd get a similar punishment to the other night—a little spanking and lots of orgasms. And while her punishment would probably involve some spanking and she'd eventually get to come, it wasn't all I had in store for her this time.

"You sure about that, Sweetheart?" I stopped as I reached her face, bracing my arms on either side of her head.

She lifted her chin. "I can take it." *Stubborn girl.* We'd see about that.

"Your safe word is Rudolph," I said, deadly serious.

A laugh bubbled out of Lexi like she was trying to hold it in. "Oh my God, seriously? Sticking with the—" I cut her words off as I reached up and gripped her throat. Not hard enough to hurt or cut off her breath, but enough to ensure I had her undivided attention.

"I'm serious, Lexi. Now, be a good girl and tell me the safe word."

"Rudolph."

"Good girl." I smiled and released her throat. Moving down her body, I made my way to her already wet center, caressing and kissing every inch of her on my way. When I reached the apex of her thighs, I avoided her clit, causing her to buck her hips. I knew where she wanted my mouth, but I was going to take my sweet time getting there.

"Brandon, please," she whined as she propped herself up on her elbows to look down at me.

I looked up at her from between her legs. "What part of the word *punishment* don't you understand?"

Exacerbated, she threw herself back down onto the bed. "Fine, but I'd better come tonight or we're going to have a real fucking problem."

Whack. My right hand came down quickly, slapping her right on the clit, causing her to cry out in a moan. "Oh, fuck."

I chuckled and then moved back between her legs. Even though she was still being a brat, I gave her a taste of what she craved and swiped my tongue through her center, earning me an appreciative hum. I continued to lap at her dripping pussy, drinking down everything she gave to me. I nipped at her clit and then took it into my mouth, sucking gently. She was squirming all over and moaning, so I knew she was close. I waited until she was right on the brink of an orgasm, and then I popped her clit out of my mouth and turned my head to kiss her thigh gently.

A frustrated grunt came from Lexi. "What the fuck?"

"Patience, Sweetheart. Remember what I said—what do good girls get?"

"Orgasms." She sounded very annoyed, but that wasn't going to get her anywhere.

"That's right, so be a good girl and let me have my fun." I flicked her clit once again with my tongue, drawing out another moan. I pushed two fingers inside of her and rubbed my thumb over her clit. She ground into me, encouraging me to keep going. I sat up slightly so I could watch her while keeping a steady pace. I felt her tighten around me, close to another orgasm, so I let my thumb slip off of her clit and slowed the movements of my fingers.

"No!" she shouted. "Please. Brandon, let me come. I swear I'll behave. I'll do anything."

Shit, that was easier than I expected. I was prepared to edge her all damn night, but the sound of her begging me to let her come was almost enough to break me. *Almost.*

"Your pleasure belongs to me tonight, Lexi. You'll come when I say you can."

A frustrated screech cut through the room as she pounded her fists into the mattress.

"All you have to do is say, 'Rudolph,' and I'll stop."

"Never," she spat.

We'll see about that. I gripped my cock, dripping with pre-cum. Her eyes darted to watch me as I gave it a few rough strokes. "Is this what you want?" I goaded her.

"Yes, please fuck me," she begged and tried to wriggle herself closer to me.

"Baby, don't worry, I'm going to give you what you want, but you'll have to be patient." I stroked my hands up her legs and over her body gently. I continued to rub her, grazing over her nipples with my thumbs. She pushed into my touch and then tried to reach between her legs to give herself some relief. I batted her hand away, and then got up out of bed and went to the bedside table. I was going to need some reinforcements. Lexi was being too stubborn for her own good. "Get up and place your hands on the headboard, Lexi."

11

LEXI

T his mother fucker. Like, seriously, who did this guy think he was? Telling me what to do. Not letting me come. I figured my punishment would be like the last time, but this was definitely *not* like the last time. This Brandon was completely unhinged and was working my last fucking nerve. I also *really* wanted to come, so I was willing to play ball. *For now.*

Begrudgingly, I turned and crawled up the bed, placing my hands on the headboard as instructed. Brandon was in the bedside drawer, probably getting a condom, so I remained still in an attempt to be a good girl. I felt the bed sag under his weight, and then he softly caressed my ass. Not what I was expecting, but it felt so good I didn't care.

He continued to graze his hand gently over my skin, leaving a trail of goose bumps in his wake, despite it feeling like a million degrees in the room. "Can I tie you up?" he whispered into my ear.

"Say less. Damn, Brando, I would never have guessed you were such a freak in the sheets," I laughed. *Whack.* His hand came down hard on my right ass cheek, the sting lingering for a moment before he smoothed his hand over it.

"Do I need to gag you, too?" Brandon asked.

"No," I answered quickly. I didn't want to be gagged. It made me feel like I couldn't breathe and definitely wasn't for me. "I'll behave."

"Good girl." Brandon moved to my side and put a soft cuff on my wrist.

The anticipation was killing me. I was so turned on; I was sure I'd come the second he touched me again. I raised my eyes and examined the headboard. Brandon's sleek metal canopy bed was unassuming and blended in perfectly with his modern decor. But upon closer inspection, I could see the added features. Metal rings were strategically placed near the top of each bedpost. The headboard, while looking like any other industrial design, had function as well, with openings throughout where one could easily attach ropes. So, Brandon was definitely not the nice guy everyone thought he was. *Hello, naughty side!*

He expertly cuffed both of my wrists and attached them to the headboard, being careful not to stretch me too far. I arched my back and shook my ass. "Brandon, I'm gonna need you to do something. Literally anything. You're killing me here," I whined. Not my finest moment, but I didn't care. I was ready to burst.

"Don't worry, Sweetheart. I'll make you feel so good. *Eventually.*" The ominous way he said '*eventually*' had me second-guessing my willingness to be restrained. He ran his hands over my ass and down my thighs and back up and over my back. I leaned into every touch, desperate for more. His fingers lightly grazed over my dripping pussy and drug my wetness over my asshole. I clenched automatically. "Has anyone ever fucked you here?" he asked, sounding too casual.

"Yes," I breathed and pushed further into his touch.

"That's a pity. Did you like it?" he asked, as I heard the click of what I assumed was a bottle of lube opening.

"Not particularly," I answered honestly. I'd tried anal a few times, but wasn't a fan. I'd push through, and as long as I had some clitoral stimulation, I could deal with it.

"I'm not going to fuck your ass tonight, but when I do, it'll be because you begged me to. And you'll love every minute of it." He sounded pretty confident, but I wasn't convinced. I jumped as cool lube drizzled onto my lower back and down my ass crack.

"I thought you said—" My words died in my mouth as he started to massage around my tight hole.

"I said I wasn't going to *fuck it*, but I want to play. Is that okay with you?" he growled. I nodded my head.

"Use your words, Sweetheart."

"Yes," I answered breathlessly.

Then, one of his thick fingers breached my entrance. I winced, but didn't pull away. Intrigued, I wondered what he had in store for me.

"So tight, baby," he said as he slowly pumped his finger

in and out of me. A moan escaped me. "Does that feel good, Sweetheart?"

I purred my approval and pushed my ass back, silently begging for more. Somehow, I was so on edge and needy that even anal was looking good to me at that moment.

Whack. His other hand came down hard on my left ass cheek, causing my muscles to tighten. "Use your words, Lexi."

"Yes. It feels so good," I moaned, surprising myself, because it somehow wasn't a lie.

"Hmmm, perfect. I want to make you feel good." He added more lube and removed his finger. Then something else teased at my entrance while he reached around me to stroke my clit with his other hand. His touch immediately sent me right back on the edge of an orgasm, but he kept the pressure light and my orgasm out of reach.

"Oh, God, please. Brandon, I need more." I barely recognized the words I was saying. I was so needy. My center ached and begged to be filled.

Whatever was pressed against my ass inched forward, and my breath hitched, and I clenched my cheeks. "Breathe, baby," Brandon instructed and added a little more pressure to my clit. "Relax. I've got you."

I released my breath and tried my best to relax, but whatever was going in my ass wasn't his finger, and the pressure was almost too much. Brandon continued to reassure me. "You're doing so well. Almost there." As I was about to tap out, the worst was over and the object pushed past my tight ring of muscle and was seated comfortably-ish inside of me. I breathed a sigh of relief. "Such a good fucking girl, Lexi. You doing okay?" His praise washed over me like a warm blanket, soothing me.

"Yeah, I'm okay. I feel so full." It was then that I realized Brandon wasn't touching me, and I turned my head to see what he was up to.

"Eyes on the headboard, Lexi," he scolded. The buttplug in my ass came to life, jolting me forward.

"What the fuck?" I gasped.

Brandon ran his hand over my hip and down the curve of my ass. "Easy, Baby. Just breathe."

After the initial shock of the vibration, I settled into the feeling and relaxed. Brandon must have noticed the change in me, because I was rewarded with his deft fingers returning to my clit. *Oh, fuck, yes.* I moaned my approval. His fingers picked up the pace and then again, when I was on the edge of an orgasm, he withdrew. *Fuck!*

"Brandon!" I shouted in protest.

"What, Sweetheart? Tell me what you need."

"I need to come. Please. I'm so close."

"You'll come on my cock, and when I tell you to. Understood?"

I nodded vigorously. "Yes. Only when you say. Please give me your dick." I was practically hysterical. I squeezed my eyes close and a single tear broke free. *What the fuck?*

The vibration in my ass increased, causing me to clench down. My pussy ached to be filled. I was about to beg again when I felt him at my entrance. *Oh shit.* Listen, Brando had a massive cock, and with the buttplug seated firmly in my ass, I wasn't sure if I could take him too. Then he pushed in slowly, filling me completely. He groaned, "Fuck, baby."

"Oh, fuuuuck," I moaned so loudly I was sure his neighbors heard me. He stayed like that, with his cock filling my pussy, vibrating buttplug humming away in my ass, his hands tightly gripping my hips. It could have been seconds or minutes, but it felt like an eternity. I needed him to move, so I wriggled a bit, earning me another smack on my ass, causing my pussy to tense, squeezing his cock.

"Damn, baby, you keep gripping me like that and this is going to be over a lot sooner than I planned."

"Good. Fuck me, Brandon, please!" I didn't care how desperate I sounded. At that point, I needed to come like I needed air to breathe.

"So impatient." He started moving, slowly at first. He reached around and touched my clit with feather-light strokes that weren't enough. As his pace increased, I climbed higher and higher, so close to the orgasm I was sure was going to ruin me for any man I'd fuck in the future. "God, Lexi. You're perfect. Look at this ass. You're such a good girl, so beautiful. You take my cock so well."

If he kept talking like that, I'd be coming soon and prayed that he'd continue. "Please, Brandon. Don't stop. Please!" I begged him.

His fingers, which were barely grazing my clit, increased their pressure, and I was on the edge again. "Don't you dare come until I tell you to," Brandon warned as his pace increased again. I could feel his engorged cock swell, filling me even more. He continued to pound into me, hitting all the right spots.

"I can't. I'm going to…" I was panting and sobbing now, so close, but trying to stop myself from tipping over the edge.

"Now, Lexi. Come for me, Sweetheart."

And I fucking did. *Holy mother of God, did I come.* I came so hard I saw stars. My whole body convulsed. I was screaming, moaning, and cursing. The orgasm was other-worldly and seemed to last for an eternity. Brandon soon followed me over the edge, cursing through his own release. The vibration in my ass stopped, the buttplug disappeared, and then he quickly released my wrists from the restraints. Completely boneless, my upper body collapsed onto the bed.

12

BRANDON

Lexi was incredible. She was everything that I wanted in a partner. She was funny, smart, beautiful, and our sexual chemistry was off the charts. I stared in awe of her as her chest fell to the bed, ass still up in the air. *Fuck, I'd never tire of that view,* I thought as I moved to scoop her up. I needed to get her cleaned up before she passed out.

As I rolled her towards me, she had a goofy smile on her face, clearly cum drunk. "That was ah-mazing," she slurred.

"*You* were amazing," I responded honestly and kissed her temple, still slick with sweat. Reaching behind her, I lifted her and carried her to my en suite. I thought about drawing a bath and washing her, but that didn't seem like something Lexi would be into at this stage of our relationship. Not that she would use that word to describe whatever we were to one another, either. I thought better of the more intimate act and turned on the shower with her still in my arms.

When the water was warm, I stepped into the shower, letting the spray wash over us both. "Mmmm, that feels nice," Lexi said before seeming to come to her senses and attempting to push me away. "Let me down, Brando." I did as she asked and gently set her down, making sure she was steady on her feet.

"Are you okay?" I asked, curious about where her head was at.

She reached past me for my body wash and squeezed a healthy portion into her palm. "Yeah, I'm fine," she answered plainly, not meeting my eyes.

I gripped her chin softly and tilted her head so she had to look me in the eyes. "Are you sure?"

She twisted her chin out of my grasp. "Yeah, I said I'm fine." She started washing herself and then continued, "Listen, I'm okay, really, that was hot. I haven't come like that in a long time."

"You've come like *that* before?" I teased, raising an eyebrow.

"Fine. Okay, I guess not. I'll give you that. You, my friend, can fuck," she chuckled as her soapy hands moved over her curves. She turned away from me, and my eyes followed the water and bubbles trailing down over her ass. *Fuck, maybe this was a mistake.* My brain wanted to talk about things, but my cock had other ideas.

"Is that what we are, Lexi? Friends?" I asked as I crowded her, my cock pressing into her back.

She spun around, her eyes wide. "How are you ready to

go again?" She shook her head as if trying to focus. "Listen, we need to talk."

I winced, hoping she wouldn't shut things down before we even had a chance to start something.

She pointed back and forth between the two of us. "This shouldn't have happened. I promised Daphne I wouldn't, but I can't seem to help myself with you."

"The feeling is mutual, I assure you," I beamed back at her.

She placed a hand on my chest. "Don't get ahead of yourself, buddy. This can't be anything serious. I'll admit, I'd like to keep you in the rotation, but you need to know I don't do feelings or relationships. If you want to fuck again, I'm in. Otherwise, this ends here and now."

I laughed, but I had the feeling she was being dead serious. *Keep me in the rotation? Nope.* If she were with me, I would not be sharing her. I leaned into her, causing her to back up, pressing her back onto the cool tile of the shower. "I don't share, Sweetheart." Reaching between us, I cupped her center. "If you're fucking me, this is mine and no one else's."

She jutted her chin up at me and pushed me back. "Fine. But when this thing has run its course, and it will, we both walk away. Don't go falling for me, because I'm not interested."

"Noted." I wondered if she'd been hurt before, and that's why she was so anti-relationships, but I had a feeling that digging deeper to find out was going to be nearly impossible. She didn't seem like the sharing type, although she intrigued me, and I wanted to peel back all of her layers.

She quickly rinsed herself and then moved to get out of the shower. As I grabbed her arm to stop her, she glowered back at me. I don't think I'd ever seen someone actually *glower* before that moment. I released her and raised my hands in surrender. "Easy, Sweetheart."

"I've gotta go, Brando. Let's not make it weird."

"How am I making it weird?" I asked.

"By trying to get me to stay. Come to think of it, that's another rule. No sleepovers." She ticked off each rule on her fingers. "No sleepovers, no feelings, no telling anyone. Oh, and no romantic shit." Still standing at the entrance of the shower, beads of water trailing down her curves, she looked sexy as hell.

"Is there a rule that says I can't tell you how goddamned beautiful you are?" I couldn't stop the words as they spilled from my mouth.

"Fucking hell, Brando." She rolled her eyes and then turned to step out of the shower, waving her hand in my direction. "I'm leaving. Message me about the tattoo. I still want to do that."

This fucking woman.

13

LEXI

What in the actual fuck did I agree to? Exclusive fucking rights? I must have been dickmatized out of my mind to agree to that. Sure, I had fuck buddies in the past, but even then, we were never really exclusive. Brandon was infuriating. He drove me fucking crazy, but I couldn't stay away.

When I got home, Daphne was on my couch. *Oopsie.* She had been spending so much time at Nathan's that I almost forgot she was still technically staying with me.

"Hey, stranger. I didn't think I'd see you tonight," I said as I discarded my purse at the door and then plopped down beside her on the couch.

"Yeah, we didn't really get to talk today at work, so I thought I'd come by. I should've texted you, though. I didn't realize you had plans tonight." Daphne was looking into her lap and wringing her hands. *Shit. Did she know where I was tonight? Did that bitch Amanda tattle on me?* "Anyway, I wanted to talk to you."

"What's up, Daphs? You're kinda freaking me out. Is everything okay?" *Play it cool, Lexi.*

"So, Nathan asked me to move in with him." She winced, waiting for my reaction, like she thought I might be upset.

"Well, duh. I figured that was coming," I joked. Anyone with eyes could see how happy they were together. Of course, they were going to move in together. "God, I thought someone died." I put a hand on my chest, relieved that it wasn't about me and Brandon. I sent a silent apology to Amanda for that bitch comment. *Love you, girl!*

Daphne slapped my arm. "Oh, my God. I was so worried about telling you. I thought you'd say it was too soon."

"Everything has happened too soon, but that seems to be par for the course with you two. Honestly, I'm surprised you lasted this long without making it official."

"So you're not mad?" Daphne asked.

"Mad? Why would I be mad? I love you, and if Nathan makes you happy, I love him, too. But if he fucks this up, I will absolutely castrate him."

"Oh, believe me, he's aware," Daphne laughed. "He knows you're a little unhinged."

I acted like I was offended, but took that as a compliment. "How dare he!" We both laughed, and I leaned over and wrapped my arms around her, squeezing her tight. "I love you, hooker."

She returned my aggressive hug. "I love you too, Lex. You'll always be my number one boo."

"Ditto." I released her, went to the kitchen, and poured myself a glass of wine. "Want a drink, or are you moving right this minute?"

Daphne chuckled. "Yeah, I'll have one. I'm staying here tonight unless you have a hot date." I almost choked on the wine I was sipping. "Or did you already? That top screams, *'I'm trying to fuck.'* But it's still a little early. Was he geriatric, and you got the early bird special?"

"Har, har, har. Very funny." *Was I really going to lie right to my best friend's face? Nope. Time to change the subject.* "So when are you making it official with Nate Dog?"

"Ugh, I hate when you call him that." Daphne's eyes shot dramatically to the ceiling. "Well, I wanted to talk to you first, but right away. Aren't you excited to get me off of your couch?"

"I love having you here, babe, but you haven't been here much anyway since you met lover boy. As long as you'll still have time for me, I'm happy for you."

"I'll always have time for you." Daphne reached over and gave my leg a squeeze. "Seriously, Lexi, you're my best friend, and I don't know what I'd do without you. You'll never get rid of me, not for a man, not for anything."

"Shut up, bitch, you're gonna make me cry." We spent the rest of the night drinking, laughing, and reminiscing about good times. Meeting Daphne at work was truly the best thing that happened to me while working there.

THE NEXT DAY, I received a message from Brandon with some dates to start my tattoo. After checking my schedule, I made an appointment for a few days later. He kept the texts tattoo-related, and I appreciated that. The last thing I needed was for him to get all weird and clingy. Hopefully, we could keep things professional at least while he was working on my tattoo. I really wanted it, and the sketch he sent me looked amazing. But this would be the most outside of the bedroom interaction I'd had with someone that I was fuck-ing, and I hoped that wouldn't complicate things to much.

On the day of my appointment, I arrived at the shop a few minutes early. There was nothing I hated more than being late. I'd rather be ten minutes early than be late for something.

The bell chimed above the door, announcing my arrival. There was a cute girl with wavy pink hair and an undercut sitting at the front desk. She looked up as I entered and offered me a sweet smile. "Hey, welcome in. Do you have an appointment?" she asked.

"Hey, yeah. I have an appointment with Brandon," I answered.

"Okay. You can have a seat, and I'll let him know that you're here." I sat in one of the leather chairs in the waiting area and watched her go back to Brandon's station. He was hunched over his table, facing away from the door, and appeared to be working on a sketch. Miss Pink Hair leaned over him and put her hand on his back. My skin felt a swift rush of heat, and my chest tightened. Suddenly, I didn't feel so good.

When I thought I might actually throw up, Brandon turned his head and smiled at me. A big, dumb smile took over his entire face, and it must have been contagious or something because I beamed back at him like an idiot. *Gross.* I quickly fixed my face as Brandon waved me over. Miss Pink Hair returned to the front and told me I could go back as I was getting up, and I gave her my fakest smile as I breezed past her.

"Hey Lexi. How are you?" Brandon asked as I approached. When I was close enough, I paused. If Brandon were a friend, I'd hug him. If he were a stranger, I'd probably shake his hand. But he and I were something else entirely, and I didn't know how to act while we both had our clothes on. As I was glitching out, Brandon solved my internal struggle by pulling me into a semi-awkward side hug. I closed my eyes and let his scent wash over me. *Dammit, he smelled good.* Like the shower gel from his apartment, warm and woodsy. The scent brought me immediately back to the other night.

I don't know how long I stayed there in his embrace, but it must have been too long. Brandon cleared his throat, causing me to jump out of his arms. "You okay there, Sweetheart?" he asked with a smirk.

I growled under my breath, "I swear to God, Brandon, you'd better stop calling me that."

"Yeah, I don't think that's going to happen," he laughed.

"Come on. Let's get to work." He motioned for me to sit in his chair. "Let me show you what I'm thinking and then you can tell me if we need to tweak anything, okay?"

"Okay, sounds good." I tried my best to relax. Brandon had an uncanny ability to set me on edge. This *Sweetheart* shit was one of the many things he did that infuriated me. The others were mostly related to his ridiculous good looks and giant cock. Why would someone's good looks and monster cock infuriate me, you ask? Because it made him practically irresistible, that's why. And I wanted more than anything to be able to resist this man.

Brandon shuffled through some papers and then turned to show me a few sketches. My jaw dropped. They were so much more detailed and vibrant than the pictures he had sent me before. One sketch in particular caught my eye. It depicted a woman from the side, with the tattoo from the other sketches wrapped around her leg. The woman looked remarkably like me. Of course, it was only a sketch from the waist down, but I'd swear it was me. I absentmindedly traced my finger over the curve of her hip. "It's beautiful," I whispered.

Unaware of my state of awe, Brandon asked, "You really like it? We can change the colors or placement if you want. If you'd rather have it on the other side—"

I interrupted, blurting out, "No, it's perfect!" Looking into his eyes was a colossal mistake, as I said, "I love it."

"Great." He placed the sketchbook down and moved to retrieve something on the side of his desk. "Because of where it will be, you'll have to remove your pants and probably your underwear too. I have this screen for privacy, and I'll keep you covered as much as possible. Is that okay with you?" He was being so professional that I *almost* forgot this man had been balls deep in me just days ago. *Almost.*

"Yeah, that's fine. I'm not exactly shy," I joked.

"Yeah, I didn't think you were, but I still don't want the whole shop staring at your ass," he said through a clenched jaw, then set up the privacy screen to block his station from the rest of the shop. "Here's a sheet to cover yourself. Wrap it around your lower half with the opening to the right. I'll step out to give you some privacy."

He gave me a small smile and then stepped around the screen, leaving me alone with my thoughts. This man had seen—*and licked*—just about every inch of me and was giving me privacy? I felt more at ease by the minute. I had been so worried about things being weird between us, but it appeared as though I was the only one feeling weird about any of this.

I quickly undressed from the waist down and wrapped the sheet around my lower half as instructed, and then hopped back up onto the table. After a few minutes, Brandon called from outside the screen, "Lexi, are you decent?"

"I don't know if that's a word I'd use to describe me," I called back. "But yes, I'm ready."

Brandon chuckled and came back into the space carrying a large sheet of thin paper with my tattoo blown up on it. "I need to check the sizing. Can you stand up for me?"

I did as he asked, and he squatted down next to me. "I'm

going to have you open the sheet slightly for me to check the size." Following his directions again, I parted the sheet just enough, keeping my intimate bits covered. He kept his eyes focused on his work. All the while, I was on freaking fire. Having him this close to me while I was practically naked from the waist down was proving to be extremely difficult for me. His breath caused goosebumps to pebble my skin, and a shiver ran through me.

Brandon reached out and placed his hand on mine. "Are you cold?"

I exhaled deeply. "No, I'm fine," I replied, trying to keep my voice steady and normal.

"I need to adjust this a bit. Have a seat, and I'll be right back. Can I get you anything? Water? Coffee?"

"No thanks. I'm okay for now," I answered and then hopped back up on the table.

"Okay. Be right back." Brandon disappeared behind the screen.

Lexi, get your shit together. He's just a man, and you are a strong, independent woman. Be cool, bitch. This was the point where I'd usually be texting or calling Daphne to talk me down. But nooo, I had to go and promise her I wouldn't get involved with Brandon, and now I'd gone and fucked myself into a corner. *Literally.* Sure, I could message her about some fictitious guy, but I didn't want to lie to her, and simply withholding the information somehow felt a little less dishonest.

Brandon returned, and we repeated the same steps. I stood up and opened the sheet, but this time, he seemed satisfied with the stencil sizing. "I think this size should work. Once I lay it down, I'll have you check it out in the mirror. If you want me to make any changes, just let me know."

He took his time applying the stencil, making sure all the tentacles lay where he wanted them to. Once he'd finished, he leaned back to take in his handiwork. "Okay, that looks perfect to me, but what do you think?" He motioned toward the full-length mirror nearby.

Keeping the sheet covering my front, I let the rest fall away as I took in the sight of my soon-to-be new ink. My mouth fell open, but no words came out. It was so fucking cool. I turned left and right, inspecting every angle. One tentacle wrapped around my thigh in the front, another stretched partway onto my lower stomach, and another one circled my leg to the back under my ass cheek. The rest of the tentacles trailed down the side of my leg. Even though this was just the outline, I knew it was going to be gorgeous when it was finished.

Brandon came closer. He reached out and pulled the sheet back up to cover my ass. "If this is going to work, I'm going to need you to keep that ass of yours covered."

My cheeks flamed, and I quickly grabbed the sheet from him. I was so captivated by the stencil; I hadn't even realized I'd exposed myself. "Sorry, it's just. It's so beautiful, Brandon, truly. I love it."

Brandon's eyes met mine through the mirror, and he gave me a grin. "Good, I'm glad. Now, let's get started."

I settled myself back on the table, making myself as

comfortable as possible. Brandon had warned me that this tattoo would require several sessions and that the first appointment could be pretty long and uncomfortable. After he had prepared his supplies, he positioned me and then asked, "Ready?"

I let out a shaky breath, feeling more nervous now that we were about to get started. "Yeah. I'm ready."

"Okay. If you need a break, let me know. If at any time it's too much, please tell me." His left hand rested on my thigh near my knee, grounding me.

I nodded and gave him a tight smile as his tattoo machine buzzed to life. It sounds funny, but the moment the needle touched my skin, I relaxed. I guess for me, the buildup was worse than the actual tattooing.

Brandon was a true artist. As I watched him work, I was mesmerized. His focus was solely on the task at hand, with no inkling that he was as affected by what he was doing as I was. Although his touch was very professional, it set me ablaze. His brows furrowed as he concentrated, and the way his tongue peeked out from the side of his mouth as he worked was utterly adorable.

There was no way I was going to make it through several sessions of this. His touch tortured me. I wanted him so fucking bad, and he was just trying to do his job.

14

BRANDON

Lexi's face said it all, but she was apparently too stubborn to admit that she was in pain. I glanced up at her again, for what felt like the hundredth time since I had started. Her eyes were closed, her brow furrowed. *Fuck.* The last thing I wanted to do was hurt her. Some people enjoyed getting tattooed, while others did not. I had hoped Lexi was the former.

I sat back and clicked off my machine. "Are you okay, Lexi? Do you need a break?" We had only just started, but she looked like she was being tortured.

Her eyes popped open, and her expression relaxed. "Oh, no, I'm good."

"Are you sure? You look like you're in pain. If you need a break, it's no problem," I offered.

She placed her hand on mine, still resting on her thigh. "I'm good. Promise."

"Okay, but if you need a break, you gotta let me know."

Damn, she was a stubborn one. I turned the machine on again and got back to work. She set her head back and closed her eyes again while I did my best to keep focused on the task at hand. I'd never been that distracted during a session before. Don't get me wrong, I always tried to be in tune with how my clients were tolerating the process and check in with them frequently, but with Lexi, I was hyper-aware of everything she did: her furrowed brow, her deep breathing, her tight lips.

I continued to outline the octopus, paying close attention to Lexi's reactions but also trying to curb my desire for her. Getting turned on while tattooing a client wasn't something that had ever happened before, and I wasn't sure how to deal with that. She had me so fucked up. I wanted to say *'fuck this tattoo'* and take her right there on the table. But I kept my touches professional, trying not to caress her leg when I had to touch it for support. When I got to the part that came across her stomach, I was so close that I swore I could smell her arousal. Or was that a memory from the other night?

She let out a soft—*was that a moan? Or was she in pain?*

"How you doin', Sweetheart?" I asked, so close that my breath caused goosebumps to pebble her skin. *Shit.* She wasn't in pain; she was turned on, too.

"Mmm, I'm good," she definitely moaned that time. My hand trailed down her thigh, stopping behind her knee. She hummed and leaned into my touch.

"Sweetheart, I'm gonna need you to stop doing that if

you want this tattoo to look good," I chuckled, and then I sat up and turned off my machine. "You know, you're very distracting."

Her eyes popped open again, as if she'd only just remembered where she was. "Shit, sorry. I kinda zoned out there for a bit."

"Listen, be a good girl and stay very still until we're done. Remember what good girls get?" I said in a hushed tone. *No one in the shop needed to hear our conversation.*

Her eyes widened as she realized what I was offering.

"Can you do that for me, Lexi? Can you be a good girl?"

She nodded and lay back. After adjusting myself— *because holy hard-on*—I turned my machine back on.

THE OUTLINE TOOK several hours to complete with minimal interruptions for water, a snack, and a bathroom break. Lexi had been on her best behavior and deserved her reward.

By the time we were finished, everyone had gone for the day. I took my time cleaning her freshly tattooed skin.

"All finished for today. Wanna take a look?" I gestured toward the mirror.

"Already? Damn, that wasn't bad at all." She jumped up off the table, wrapping the sheet loosely around herself. As she stood in front of the mirror and let the sheet fall open, she grinned. I moved to stand behind her as she examined my work.

"Do you like it?" I asked.

She looked up at me through the mirror. "Like it? Brandon, I fucking love it." The smile that broke out over her face was so real, I couldn't help but return it with my own.

"I'm glad." I turned and patted the table. "Now hop back up so I can cover it."

"Yes, sir," she purred. *Oh fuck me, that went straight to my dick.* Since I told her to be a good girl, I'd been able to keep *him* in check, but since her tattoo was finished, all bets were off, apparently. I made quick work of covering her tattoo with SecondSkin.

"Is anyone else here?" she asked as she propped herself up on her elbows.

"It's just us," I answered in a growl.

"Well, was I a good girl?" she asked, and then bit her lower lip. As if summoned by the devil himself, my dick strained against the zipper of my jeans.

Let me preface this next part by saying I had never fucked someone in my shop. Up until that moment, the thought of doing so had never even crossed my mind. I mean, it's gotta be some sort of health code violation or something, right? Didn't matter—I was about to give Lexi her much-deserved reward.

"You were such a good girl, Lexi." I pulled on the sheet slightly to expose her.

She gasped and brought her hand to her mouth, feigning shock. "Oh my God, what are you doing? I just came in here for a tattoo." She tried to keep a straight face but failed. "This seems very unprofessional." She was so damn cute.

My gaze drifted between her legs, and I think my heart stopped. I'd seen her bare before, but seeing her like this, in this environment, hit differently. I licked my lips and ran a hand up the inside of her non-tattooed thigh, stopping before the apex. She leaned into the touch and made a sound that almost unraveled what was left of my self-control.

"Patience, Sweetheart."

She rolled her eyes. "Ever heard of a quicky? You know, wham, bam, thank you ma'am?"

I couldn't help the laugh that burst out of me. "Jesus, Lexi. Can't a guy take his time and enjoy watching you squirm a little before getting you off?" I continued to stroke her everywhere but where she wanted me. "Don't be a brat. You know what happens when you are."

"What, you'll make me come even harder? Oh, darn."

Fucking Lexi—always with the sass. Then it was my turn to roll my eyes. While I wanted to torture her some more and drag this out, her smart ass mouth had me painfully hard and unable to hold myself back anymore.

I leaned down and, without warning, swiped my tongue through her center and then nipped her thigh. "Hmm, so wet for me," I murmured against her leg.

"Yes, Brandon, please. I need to come."

"Already?"

"I've wanted this all day," she confessed.

"Really?"

She closed her eyes before she spoke again, like she couldn't look me in the eye to say what she needed to say. "Yes. As much as it pains me to admit, Brandon, I am very attracted to you, and having you touch me all day with no payoff has been absolute torture." Her eyes opened. "Now, I'm gonna need you to let me come. I've been a good girl, and I think we both deserve it."

She made a pretty convincing argument, so I dove back in between her legs, taking my time to keep her right on the edge. She squirmed beneath my touch as I worked her to the brink and then backed off again.

"Please," she begged.

Without warning, I nipped her clit and sucked it into my mouth. Her hips bucked off the table, and she cried out. I thrust two fingers into her, causing her to come hard, soaking my face and the table below her.

"Oh my God, Brandon, fuck!" she screamed, but I didn't let up. I kept finger fucking her right into another forceful orgasm while continuing my clit focused assault.

After she'd come a few more times, she tried to push me away. "Stop. Please, Brandon, it's too much."

I removed my fingers from her dripping center and continued to lap at her lazily, letting her come down slightly.

"Damn, Brando. You can eat some pussy," she said breathlessly.

I grinned against her skin. "Baby, I could eat this pussy all day. Fucking delicious," I growled before standing up.

She looked cum drunk—her eyes glassy and hooded, with a lazy smile plastered on her face. "Get up," I ordered. "I'm not finished with you yet."

Her eyes widened, but she complied. Slowly moving to

stand on shaky legs. I wove my hand into her hair, giving her a firm tug to angle her face towards mine. She smiled up at me before I attacked her mouth with mine. The kiss was ravenous, as if we were two starved people, hungry for each other alone. My other hand reached around her to bring her closer. My dick was so hard, begging to be released from the confines of my jeans.

I broke our kiss and spun her around suddenly, causing her to let out a small gasp. I placed a hand on her back and pushed her chest down onto the table. After briefly making sure her freshly tattooed skin wasn't up against the table, I kicked her legs out slightly. She arched her back, pushing her ass up towards me.

"Look at you, Sweetheart. So ready for this dick, aren't you?" I kept one hand on her back and used the other to free my cock.

"Yes, please, Brandon, I want you to fuck me," she professed, without a hint of brattiness. I removed a condom from my pocket and opened it with my teeth before rolling it over myself.

I leaned down over her, my chest against her back, and breathed into her ear, "Hold on, baby. I've been thinking about doing this all damn day."

15

———————

LEXI

*F*uck me. I'd been wound so tight all day, and with one swipe of this man's tongue, I completely unraveled. Brandon licked me until I begged him to stop, then bent me over the table where he had spent the day tattooing me, and fucked me within an inch of my life. Seriously, it was *that* good.

After what felt like my millionth orgasm, I got the fuck out of there in true Lexi fashion. The last thing I needed was to give Brandon the wrong impression of me and my intentions. We had discussed the rules, but I needed to *show* him I meant them with my actions. If what Daphne said about him was true, I didn't need to be sending this guy mixed signals. I didn't want to lead him on and end up being the heartless bitch who broke the nice guy's heart.

Heartless? Was that what I was? I mean, I loved my mom, and I loved Daphne. I had love for other people in my life, too, *didn't I?* Zoning out at a local coffee shop, waiting for my order, it hit me. My circle was so small. All of this not letting people in shit was keeping me from even making friends. My goal was to not fall in love and have to deal with that heartbreak, but it was also costing me a full and healthy social life. Now that Daphne was joined at the hip with Nathan, my circle was even smaller.

"Dirty chai latte for Lexi!" the barista called, interrupting my spiraling thoughts. I grabbed my drink and went to sit by the window. It had started snowing this morning, and I was excited to take it all in, even though winter wasn't my favorite season. I preferred warmer weather, fewer layers of clothing, and sunshine, but I could appreciate the beauty of fresh snowfall. The way it coated the city in a blanket of white. I'd be lying if I didn't secretly hope for a white Christmas every year.

It had been a few days since my tattoo, and I was itching to see Brandon again. As if he could somehow hear my thoughts, my phone chimed with an incoming text from him.

BRANDON

Hey, just wanted to check in and see how your tattoo was healing.

ME

So far, so good. That skin stuff is starting to lift. I know you said to leave it for a few days, but do you think it's okay if I take it off today?

BRANDON

Yeah, that should be fine. We should schedule your next session. With Christmas coming up, I want to make sure I get you on the books.

Shit. Christmas. I hadn't even thought about that yet. I usually spent holidays with my mom or Daphne or both of them, but this year had sort of flown by, and I hadn't made any solid plans yet. Thanksgiving had been Mom and me and a tiny little turkey. It was perfect, but she let me know she planned on working on Christmas this year, so I needed to find something else to do. *Crap.*

I was used to being alone and doing things solo, but the holidays were different. I didn't enjoy being alone, and I needed to figure something out. Worst-case scenario, I could probably pick up a shift at the hospital.

I ignored Brandon's text and pulled up my message thread with Daphne.

ME

Hey, what are your plans for Christmas?

DAPHNE

We're doing Christmas Eve at Nathan's dad's and Christmas Day with my parents. I thought you were hanging with your mom?

ME

She's working. I totally forgot.

DAPHNE

Would you want to come to Nathan's
dad's for dinner? I'm sure he wouldn't
mind. He's really cool.

DAPHNE

I'd invite you to my parents', but I was
hoping they could get some more one-on-
one time with Nathan.

Did I want to hang out with Brandon's family? That felt
like crossing a line, but, on the other hand, we were bound
to be put in these types of situations if he and I continued
our little arrangement. Plus, Daphne and Nathan seemed
like the real deal. *Fuck it.*

ME

Okay, I'm in as long as his dad is okay
with me crashing the party.

DAPHNE

Yay! It'll be nice to have some more
estrogen in that house for once. I'll ask
and get back to you, but I'm sure it'll be
fine. See ya at work tomorrow?

ME

Unfortunately.

DAPHNE

ME

I backed out of our messages and reopened my thread with Brandon.

ME

> Okay, let me know when you want me to come in, and I'll check my schedule.

BRANDON

> Would it be out of the question for you to come in on Christmas Eve morning? If you have plans, we can do it another day, but I'm booked until after New Year's right now.

ME

> Funny you mention Christmas Eve, because Daphne sort of invited me to your dad's place for dinner that night.

BRANDON

> That's perfect! We can work on your tattoo beforehand, and then I can drive you.

This seemed too much like a date, but I decided I needed to just go with it. We had set our boundaries—*or at least I had*—and I needed to trust that Brandon would respect them.

ME

> Okay, sounds like a plan. Let me know what time you want me at the shop.

BRANDON

> Will do.

BRANDON

That's two weeks away, though. Will I see
you before then? 😊

Subtle.

ME

I'm sure you will. Bring condoms to the
hospital. I want to get railed by Santa for
real.

BRANDON

My cheeks hurt from smiling, so I quickly fixed my
face. There was no way in hell I was gonna be one of *'those
girls'*—acting all gaga while texting a boy. The thought of
repeating our little Grey's Anatomy-esque hookup had me
practically bubbly, which was so unlike me, but whatever. I
guess extraordinary dick made me giddy.

After placing my phone back in my bag, my gaze
returned to the view outside the coffee shop. From this
vantage point, I had an excellent spot to do some serious
people-watching. I was only a few blocks from my apartment, nearer to shops and businesses. It was a weekday, and
the street was bustling with people, probably on their lunch
breaks, getting in some holiday shopping.

With only two weeks until Christmas, the non-procrasti-
nators likely had their shopping well underway. I, on the
other hand, was a Grade A procrastinator. I did my best
work under pressure in most situations, and shopping for
gifts was no different. Besides, I only really ever shopped

for Daphne and my mom, so it wasn't like it took me long to accomplish. But I didn't buy just *any* gift. It had to be the right gift for the right person. I'd rather give them nothing at all than give some useless bobble that would sit and collect dust on a shelf, or even worse, end up being re-gifted.

I spent some more time enjoying the snowfall and people-watching while sipping on my latte before heading back to my apartment to do some meal prepping for work. *Don't get it twisted*—I didn't do the health freak bullshit kind of meal prepping. It was just more practical to pack myself some meals and snacks for the hospital in case I was too busy to get to the cafeteria. Although, come to think of it, maybe more trips to the cafeteria were exactly what I needed.

ALL OF MY hopes and dreams of banging Santa in an on-call room evaporated when I got to work the next day only to find out we were at capacity and short-staffed. *Good thing I meal prepped, I guess.* The morning flew by, and my lunch consisted of a bag of chips at the nursing station. Yeah, I knew we weren't *supposed* to have food and drinks in patient care areas, but sue me. We had to eat when and where we could.

By mid-afternoon, management's bribes must have worked, because we finally got some extra nurses in to help us. As soon as someone came to offer me a break, I ran for the bathroom, followed by a trip to the break room to sit and eat something more substantial. Unfortunately, I still had hours left in my shift.

Amanda was in the break room, and after getting my lunch bag from the fridge, I joined her at her table.

"Hey, girl. How you holdin' up?" I asked as I plopped down in my chair.

"Fuck, Lexi. Today's brutal," she answered as she took a huge bite of her sandwich. Probably trying to shovel as much in as she could before we were inevitably interrupted. *Smart girl.*

"Yeah, I hate it when we're so short. I mean, it's ICU, for fuck's sake. How are we supposed to keep these patients safe without help?" There was no time to hop up on my soapbox. Every minute of my break was precious. I needed to eat, pee again, and get back out there.

Between bites of my own subpar lunch of grapes and Triscuits—*meal prepping at its finest, ladies and gentlemen*—I pulled out my phone to do a little doom scrolling. There on my message icon was a red bubble showing a missed text. I knew who it was before I even opened the app. *Fuck.* I wanted nothing more than to say, *fuck this place* and jump Santa's bones, but that wasn't in the cards for me. I reluctantly opened my messages app and instantly regretted it. My jaw hung open as I took in the photo he had sent.

Usually, I wasn't a fan of unsolicited dick pics, but this particular dick pic was definitely getting saved in my spank bank. *Holy hell.* It was taken at his apartment in front of a full-length mirror, and he was naked except for his Santa beard and hat. He stood there looking sexy as hell, with his phone in one hand and a raging hard-on in the other. The caption read, *Santa has a present for you.*

"Fuck me," escaped my lips in a whisper, causing Amanda to perk up.

"What's wrong?" she asked, looking up at me. "Or what's right?" she laughed. I guessed my expression had given me away.

"Nothing," I said, as I quickly stuffed my phone back into my pocket.

"Liar." She put down her sandwich and turned her chair to face me. "Listen, bitch. I haven't had sex in so long that my hymen has probably regenerated itself. I need to live vicariously through you, so spill it."

Fuck it. She already knew about my little Santa rendezvous. What was the harm in keeping her in the loop? *Well, as long as Daphne didn't find out.*

"Fine. Santa sent me the hottest picture." I grinned at her. "I was supposed to meet him for a quickie today before I found out we were short."

"Can I see it?" Her eyes were wide, and I could almost see the drool gathering in her mouth.

"Absolutely not. It was meant for my eyes only. I don't think he'd appreciate my sharing it with strangers."

"Buzzkill." Amanda pouted. "So, when are you going to see him again?"

"I'm not sure. Hopefully before Christmas Eve, though. That's when I have my next tattoo session."

"Is that what you're calling your dick appointments these days?" she snorted.

Daphne rushed into the room, making a B-line for the fridge. I shot Amanda a death glare, praying she got the hint.

"Is it a fucking full moon?" Daphne hissed as she rummaged through the contents of the refrigerator.

"Triscuits?" I offered.

16

BRANDON

As soon as I sent that picture, I regretted it. I was so damn nervous. I'd never done anything like that before, and I assumed Lexi would be into it. But when she didn't reply, I started to panic. *What if I'd gone too far? What if I crossed a line?* I knew she didn't want anyone to know about us, and we had to keep things casual, but I thought she'd enjoy a little teasing via text. *How could I have read her so wrong?*

My spiraling thoughts continued throughout the morning. I did my best to stay present for the kids' sake, though. It wasn't their fault that their pseudo Santa for the day was having a mini mental breakdown. At every lull, I checked my phone, but she still hadn't seen the message by the time I took my lunch break.

When I was ready to pack up for the day, I checked again and saw that she had seen the message but still hadn't responded. *Well, fuck.* I sent another message, trying to do some damage control.

ME

Hey, sorry if that was out of line.

I hoped she wasn't too pissed about the photo, and that I could make it up to her later. But it was late afternoon, and I had to get to the shop for an appointment.

When I entered the shop, Dylan and my dad were both working on clients, and Paige, our receptionist, was at the desk. Dad had only recently come back to work after taking an '*early retirement*' after Mom died. We all sort of knew he wouldn't be able to stay retired, but supported his decision to have his time away. Coming back to the place they had built together must have been hard, but I could tell my old man was bored senseless sitting at home. And since coming back into the shop last month, he'd been all smiles.

"Hey," I raised a hand as I entered to greet everyone.

"Hey, Brandon," Paige said with a wave back. "Your appointment called and said they are running a few minutes late."

"Okay, thanks. You can send them back whenever they get here." I stopped at Dad's station near the front. "How's it going, Pops?"

He looked up over his glasses, which he only used when he was working or reading. "Pretty good, son. How was the hospital?"

"Busy today. The kids were all so excited to see me."

"You're probably making their days, Brandon. You know better than most how awful it can be being stuck in the hospital during the holidays." Dad's gaze shifted out of focus, likely recalling the countless days spent in hospitals with Mom.

"That's why I keep going back. It's hard to see the sicker kids, but the smiles on their faces make it all worth it." I glanced at his client, who was looking a little annoyed at my interruption. "Sorry, I'll let you get back to work."

"You're fine. Bill here doesn't have anywhere to be," he laughed. "Isn't that right, Bill?"

"Speak for yourself, you old fuck," Bill chuckled, clearly not as annoyed as I thought.

I moved back to my station, throwing a nod to Dylan as I passed him. My next client was for a touch-up, so I didn't really have anything to prepare for them. I sat and pulled out my sketchbook, opening it to the last page I had been working on. I stared at the image in front of me. It was one of many drawings I'd done since I first laid eyes on *her* at that club. She was a work of art all on her own, and every sketch I did seemed to fall short of capturing her beauty, but that didn't stop me from trying. Footsteps approaching had me quickly closing my sketchbook.

"Whatcha working on, bro?" Dylan asked, looking over my shoulder.

"Nothing." It wasn't like me to hide my sketches, but those were for my eyes only.

"Bullshit," he said, exaggerating the word for added effect. "Don't be so secretive. I'm not going to steal your designs. Remember, I'm the talented brother."

What an ass.

"Very funny. You done for the day?" I asked, attempting to change the subject.

"Yeah, I was thinking about heading out for a drink. When are you done? Want to join me?" he asked.

"I've got a client coming in any minute. Shouldn't take me too long, though. I'll shoot ya a text when I'm done to see what you're up to, okay?" The last thing I wanted to do was play wingman for my man whore of a brother. I'd rather end up balls deep in Lexi, but since she wasn't returning my messages, I wasn't sure that was even an option.

He slapped me on the back. "Yeah, sounds good. I'll try to save ya some pussy."

"Dylan!" Dad called from the front.

Dylan leaned down and whispered, "How the fuck did he hear that?"

"I don't know if you know this about yourself, Dylan, but you are not a quiet person," I chuckled.

"Whatever. See ya later."

"Yeah, see ya." I waved as he turned and made his way out of the shop.

My client walked in a few minutes later, and I got right to work. Avery had been a long-time client, and we were freshening up one of their older tattoos, so it didn't take me long. I loved all of my clients, but I had to admit that Avery was one of my favorites. They always had crazy ass stories from touring with their band, and I loved hearing about all the places they'd traveled to—it made the time fly by too. Before I knew it, I had finished.

"All done. Take a look and let me know if there are any spots you want me to go over." I motioned to the mirror.

Avery stood, inspected my work and then turned around with a huge grin. "Perfect as always. Thanks, Brandon."

"Always a pleasure. Glad we got to catch up. Where ya off to next?" I asked, genuinely interested and a little jealous since I hadn't ever traveled outside of the tri-state area myself.

"Taking a little break for the holidays and then we're off to the West Coast for a few shows."

"Oh, nice. Well, enjoy your time off. If you sneak in a local show, let me know. I'd love to come see you play again."

"Will do. If I don't see you before, Merry Christmas," Avery offered, and brought me in for a hug.

"You too." As they made their way to the front, I called out, "Hey, be careful out there. The snow's really coming down."

"You too."

After Avery had settled up with Paige, I sent her home for the day. The snow was sticking to the roads, and we didn't have any other appointments. With the weather getting bad, we'd probably close early anyway.

Dad was still working on his last client, so I decided I'd stay until he finished, in case someone else came in. After cleaning and packing up my station for the night, I parked myself at the front desk and finally pulled out my phone.

On the lock screen was a message from Lexi.

I quickly clicked on it to expand the message. It was a photo of Lexi, looking like a fucking goddess. Facing away from the camera, she was on her knees, with her back arched and looking over her shoulder, dressed in some black cutout lingerie. My jaw went slack as I fumbled to hide my phone out of view. It was Dad, his client, and me in the shop, but that shit was for my eyes only, and I'd have gouged out the eyes of anyone else who saw it.

After moving my phone out of sight, I leaned down and zoomed in on the shot. She was a fucking knockout. The teasing look on her face and her lip between her teeth did me in. I was a goner.

Yeah, fuck hanging with Dylan tonight. I shot him a text, letting him know I was tired and wouldn't be making it out.

17

LEXI

Fuck today. All I wanted was to sneak away at lunch for a quickie with Brandon, but *nooooooo*. We had to go, and not only be short-staffed, but busy as fuck too. The second my shift ended, I got right the fuck out of there and made my way home, not before stopping by the cafeteria to see if Brandon was still there. Unfortunately for me, he had already gone for the day.

I couldn't stop thinking about that photo he'd sent me. *Goddammit*, I'd never seen anything so hot in all of my twenty-six years. I still hadn't responded because, honestly, what the hell was I gonna say? *Nice dick?* A dick pic of that caliber deserved a better response than that. Although I did kind of feel bad that I didn't message him back. *That's okay.* I was about to make it up to him.

When I got home, I showered and then got myself ready. Nothing too crazy—a little makeup and a brush through my hair. Then I picked out one of my favorite lingerie pieces and got to work setting the mood in my room. It was time for a photo shoot of my own.

With the lights dimmed and the clutter cleared away, my room transformed into my own personal photography studio. I propped my phone up on the floor and got down on all fours. After making sure that the lighting was just right, I faced away from the camera and positioned myself on my knees. I turned to look at the camera and check the shot. *Damn, this looked hot*, I thought.

Once I was happy with everything, I set the timer on my phone and scrambled to get back into position, this time arching my ass up slightly more. It took a few tries to get the perfect shot, but boy, did I get it!

Thrilled with my handiwork, I opened up my text thread with Brandon and sent the photo. I didn't wait for his response, though, because I didn't sit by the phone for anyone, not even *Lord Big Dick Edgington* himself. So, I threw on a fluffy robe and made myself some dinner.

I'D JUST SAT down on the couch with a big glass of wine and my piping hot mac n' cheese when there was a knock on my door. I wasn't expecting anyone, and I swore to God that if it were someone trying to sell something, I'd murder them. Disgruntled that my dinner would have to wait, I set it down and went to see who it was.

"Yes?" I questioned whoever dared interrupt my first actual meal of the day. Unless you count coffee as a meal.

"Lexi, it's Brandon."

What.

The.

Fuck.

How did he know where I lived?

"What can I do for you, Brando?" I asked in my most snarky tone. While I didn't know how he found my place, I knew exactly why he was here, and I planned on making him work for it.

"Don't toy with me, woman. Open this door." He sounded like he was in no mood for my shenanigans, so I opened the door, deciding I could make him work for it inside my warm apartment.

I couldn't believe I was letting him in. First of all, I *never* had guys over at my apartment. I always went to theirs. Second, *how did he know where I lived? Was I being stalked? Was I in danger?* I laughed to myself, because while Brandon was a total freak in the sheets, he was still a really nice guy, and I didn't think he'd hurt a fly, let alone me.

Standing back to give him room to enter, he strode in, looking frazzled, and paced around my apartment. His usually perfect man bun was coming loose, and his hair was covered in thick snowflakes. He pulled out his hair tie, ran his fingers through his locks, and then pulled them back to re-secure them.

I stood there taking him in and, *fuck me*, did he look good. My nipples were already tight little peaks begging for attention, and my pussy demanded to be filled. I was going to ruin this man.

I undid the tie of my robe and let it fall to the ground. *Welp, that got his attention.* Brandon stopped in his tracks and looked me up and down. He then took three long strides to get to me, lifted me, and slammed us against the wall, careful not to actually hurt me. I wrapped my legs around him as his mouth crashed into mine.

"You're going to be the death of me, you know that, don't you?" he asked, while kissing and groping me, then pressing his erection into my pelvis. "You drive me fucking crazy."

"That picture you sent was so fucking hot," I admitted. "Please tell me you brought the Santa hat."

"It's in the car."

"Go."

That man dropped me like a bad habit and went running out of my apartment. I didn't stop laughing until he came bounding back in with the biggest shit-eating grin and the Santa hat on his head.

"You're ridiculous," I laughed. "Take off your shoes and your coat. You're getting snow everywhere."

"Oh, shit. Sorry." He kicked off his shoes and shrugged out of his jacket, hanging it by the door. Dressed in jeans and a well-fitted flannel shirt, he was giving off some serious lumberjack vibes. *Smash.*

As Brandon turned, he caught sight of my food on the coffee table. "Did I interrupt your dinner?"

I was still in my sparse lingerie, nipples standing at attention, goosebumps pebbling my flesh. I wanted to fuck, but I also needed to eat. My stomach growled its approval of the latter loud enough that I was sure Brandon heard it.

He moved quickly, picking my robe up off the floor and wrapping it around me. "Sorry, Lexi. I barged in here unannounced. Fuck, you're freezing." He rubbed his hands over my arms to warm me. *Damn, that felt so good.*

"I'm okay, really." Grabbing his shirt, I pulled him to me. "I know a way you can warm me up." My stomach growled even louder, and I winced. There was no way he didn't catch that one.

"Food first, then fucking." He gave me a wink.

"Fine, I *do* love food, too," I agreed reluctantly. "Are you hungry?"

"Yeah, I could eat. If you have enough for two, that is."

I moved into the kitchen—already missing his touch—and portioned out another bowl of mac n' cheese. "You want a glass of wine?"

"No, I'm not much of a wine guy. Water is fine."

I returned to the living room and set down his water and food and then sat on the couch cross-legged. It had only been a short while since I'd abandoned my own food, so thankfully, it was still warm enough to dig right in.

"So, Brando, how'd you get my address?" I questioned in between bites.

He chuckled, "From your form at the shop."

"Are you even allowed to do that?" I pointed my fork at him and arched an eyebrow. "What's a tattoo shop equivalent to HIPAA? You've got to be violating something like that."

He laughed. "I mean, I wouldn't give out your info to a stranger, but it's my shop, and I just so happened to see your address when you filled out the form."

"Yeah, right. *Just so happened to see it*? Sure."

"Are you upset that I'm here?" he asked seriously.

"Truthfully? No, I was actually hoping I'd see you tonight. That pic you sent this morning was so fucking hot." I pointed my fork back and forth between us. "But this whole eating dinner together is dangerously close to crossing a line of our arrangement."

"Eating mac n' cheese is against the rules?"

I exhaled an annoyed breath. "No, but you coming here, us sharing a meal—I don't want you getting your hopes up."

"Lexi, I have no illusions about us. I think we have great chemistry, and if that's all it is, then so be it."

"Mmmhmm." I didn't believe a word that was coming out of his mouth, and I didn't think he did either, but that was going to end up being his fucking problem, not mine.

We ate our food and made small talk while I guzzled my wine. It was bordering on a date, and I needed liquid courage to deal with that. I couldn't remember the last time I'd been on a date, if ever. Pre-fucking drinks surely didn't count.

"Can I ask you something?" Brandon asked, putting his bowl aside and turning to face me on the couch.

"I guess so," I reluctantly agreed.

"Why are you so anti-relationships? I know we sort of talked about it before, but I'm curious as to why? Did someone hurt you in the past?" *This mother fucker.*

That was not a topic I wanted to entertain. Not with him, not with anyone. *Did someone hurt me? No.* Someone hurt my mom, and I promised myself I wouldn't end up like her. This thing between us wasn't going anywhere, and I wasn't about to bare my soul to some guy who wouldn't be sticking around.

"Nope. I just like my freedom. Why buy the cow? Am I right?" I joked. "Let's change the subject, okay?"

Brandon shook his head, but agreed. "Okay, Lexi. If that's what you want." We finished our meals on safer subjects, such as my tattoo, the shop, and my job at the hospital.

After we had finished eating, I got up to put our dishes in the sink and top off my wine. When I returned to the living room, Brandon was getting real cozy and had turned on the TV.

"Excuse me, but what are you doing?"

"I thought we could watch a movie or something," he said so casually, I almost forgot he wasn't just a friend. *Almost.*

"Are you okay? Like seriously, did you hit your head on the way over here or something?" I stared blankly at him.

"What's the matter, Sweetheart? Afraid you'll catch feelings if we hang out?" Brandon countered with a smirk.

"You're an idiot." Despite the sass I was throwing at

him, I couldn't help the smile that broke out on my face. "Fuck, fine. I gotta let my mac n' cheese digest, anyway, before I do what I had planned to you."

"Oh, you have a plan?" He grinned back at me.

"I've been thinking about it all damned day, actually."

18

BRANDON

The anticipation was killing me. I couldn't wait to see what Lexi had in store for me, but I tried to focus on the TV. Since it was almost Christmas, there were tons of holiday movies to choose from, and I settled on ELF, because who didn't love that movie?

Lexi and I didn't talk much as we watched. My mind raced. I wanted to know more about her and what made her tick. *Why was she so jaded? How could I get her to open up?* My thoughts continued to spiral until she got up to go to the bathroom.

A few moments later, she called out, "Hey, Santa! Come in here."

I grabbed my Santa hat and moved quickly toward her voice. Down a small hall and past a bathroom, I arrived in Lexi's bedroom. The lighting was dim, but not so dim that the sight of her didn't stop in my tracks.

There, on the floor by the foot of the bed, was Lexi in all

of her glory, looking sexy as hell on her knees in black lingerie. *Fuck.* She was something out of a dream.

"Oh, shit," I said, somewhat surprised.

Lexi chuckled, but then got serious. "Ever since you sent me that picture, I've been thinking about this. I wanna gag on Santa's cock."

Double fuck. My dick, immediately hard, fought against the zipper of my pants. I pulled my shirt off and then put on the Santa hat. If sucking off Santa was what Lexi wanted, then that's what she was going to get.

I took a few long strides into the room until I was standing right in front of her. "You want this cock? Come and take it, Sweetheart," I demanded as I crossed my arms over my chest.

She seemed to shiver with the prospect as she reached up to undo my belt. Licking her lips, she took her time undoing my pants. I savored every moment, quite enjoying the build-up and anticipation myself.

When my painfully hard dick sprang free from the confines of my pants, a wide grin broke out on Lexi's face. Her gaze shifted to my face. "This is one impressive cock, Santa."

I chuckled. Lexi was sexy as hell, and every time we'd been together had been amazing, but she was also funny and had a way of making me laugh, even in the most intimate of situations. I grabbed her chin and pressed the head of my dick to her lips. "Have you been naughty or nice, Lexi?"

She hummed against me, causing my cock to twitch.

Her tongue darted out and licked the tip softly, all the while maintaining eye contact. "I guess you're about to find out."

With my pants around my ankles and a Santa hat on my head, she took me into her mouth, and my knees almost gave out. Each time with her was better than the time before, but I wasn't sure how that was even possible. She continued to suck, lick, and gag on my cock. My toes curled as I fought to maintain my composure, determined to let her have her way with me.

After a few more minutes of the best blow job I'd ever received, I couldn't take it anymore and wrapped her hair in my hand and started fucking her throat. She moaned and hummed around me, making me even more feral for her. I went deeper, causing her to gag again. "You're doing so well, Sweetheart." With one hand, she was massaging and teasing my balls, and the other disappeared between her legs. Ordinarily, I'd tell her to stop touching herself to delay her gratification, but in that moment, she deserved to come. "Fuck yes, Lexi. Make yourself come for me." She was bringing me so close to the edge myself, and if she wanted to fall over the edge with me, then so be it.

Her moaning became louder; her movements erratic. She was close, and so was I. I took more and more. Tears streaked down her face. She looked so beautiful. "You want me to coat your throat with my cum, baby?" She moaned and nodded around me, and that did me in.

She continued to finger fuck herself while I shot hot ropes of cum down her throat. Her fingers stopped as she came. The sight of her drinking me down while making herself come would be permanently etched into my memory. It was hands down the hottest thing I'd ever seen.

I stroked her face, running my thumb under her eye where her mascara was running down her cheek. "You're such a good girl, Lexi. That was amazing."

She popped my barely softening dick out of her mouth and grinned up at me. "So what's the verdict, Santa? Am I naughty or nice?"

"Truthfully, I think you're a little of both." I scooped her up in my arms and shuffled her to the bed, setting her down carefully.

"That's fair," she sighed into her pillow as I finally removed my pants. "What are you doing?" she asked, popping up on her elbow to look at me.

"It's cute that you think we're done for the night, Sweetheart."

Her eyes moved from mine to my dick, which was already getting hard again. "I'll give it to you. Your refractory period is impressive."

A chuckle escaped me. "I guess. Either that or it's just what you do to me. Do you know how irresistible you are?"

"No need to stroke my ego, Brando. I'm not exactly playing hard to get here," she laughed.

"Such a smart mouth on you."

"Oh, no. I guess you'll have to punish me," she cooed and rolled her eyes.

I moved quickly, but she was up and moving before I could reach her, laughing maniacally as she jumped off the bed. "Oh, I'm gonna punish you, alright."

"Gotta catch me first," she teased. She ran around the bed, and when I reached for her, she jumped back on the bed and ran to the other side. I let that go on for a short while before cutting over the bed and sweeping her up into a bear hug and falling back onto the bed with her in my arms, careful to protect her from any harm.

We were both breathless and laughing until our eyes met. The air in the room seemed hotter, *thicker*. The tension hung between us until our need for one another bubbled over and we practically attacked each other. Our mouths met in a fury of hurried kisses. My hands greedily explored her body, taking time to learn what made her moan and what she liked.

I was painfully hard again. Reaching between her legs, I tore away the thin scrap of fabric that separated us, causing her to gasp. "Hey, I liked this one!" But her protests were cut short as I strummed her clit.

"Condom?" I breathed into her.

She broke our kiss and rolled over me to retrieve a condom from her bedside table, which she wasted no time rolling over my cock. Her chest was heaving; her desire for me, *for this*, was evident on her face. Her punishment would have to wait because the sight of her like this—so full of need—had me with only one mission: to make her come all over my cock.

"How do you want it?" I asked.

She paused only for a moment before answering. "Lie on your back."

I complied quickly. She was in charge now.

Lexi moved over me, positioning her entrance above my straining cock. I thrust up, but she moved so I couldn't reach her. "Tsk. Tsk," she scolded. "Not so fast. Are you okay if I use a toy while we fuck?"

"Absolutely." I wasn't one of those guys that was intimidated when a girl used a toy to get off. I knew I could do the job myself, but if that's what she wanted to do, then I was all for it. I just wanted her to feel good.

She leaned down and kissed my nose. "Good answer." She rolled back over to the bedside table and then rolled back on top of me with a small vibrator in her hand. "Glad to see you're not intimidated by Clit Eastwood here."

I couldn't help the laugh that ripped through me, but quickly recovered, because I didn't want to kill the mood. "Not a chance. I think it's hot when you make yourself come."

"Good boy." *Oof.* I didn't think I had a praise kink, but damn if that didn't do something for me.

Lexi reached down, stroked me, and then turned around to face my feet before lifting and impaling herself on my cock. "Oh, fuuuuckkk," I moaned. This angle was next level. She rolled her hips, and I swear I almost came again right then and there.

Her little toy buzzed to life. I expected her to place it on her clit, but she turned and looked me in the eyes as she took it into her mouth. Withdrawing it with a string of saliva trailing behind, she moved it between her legs. First, rubbing it on her clit as she continued to roll her hips before moving it to glide over my balls. *Oh, fuck.*

I was no prude, and I've had my share of toy play in the bedroom, but this was the first time I'd been on the receiving end. Lexi grinned at me as I moaned my appreciation. "You like that?" she asked, knowing full well the effect she was having on me.

"Yeah, baby. That feels so good," I managed to get out before she turned away from me and started moving again, grinding her hips in into me. The toy teased where we connected, down my scrotum and back again. The sensation was amazing. Then, when she increased her pace, she slipped the device under my balls to tease the sensitive area just behind. "Oh, shit, Lexi. Fuck." I was losing any restraint that I had been desperately holding onto. It was all almost too much.

Her one hand held the toy firmly in place, massaging my taint. With her other hand, she massaged her clit, occasionally drifting down to stroke where our bodies met. I thrust up into her as she continued to fuck me. I was on the edge, but wanted to hold out until she came again, too.

"Baby, I'm going to come if you keep this up. I'm not going to last. You need to come. Now."

"Yes, Santa." She quickly placed the vibrator on her clit and started moving up and down my shaft with more determination. I could still feel the vibration, and that, paired with her pussy pulsing around me, sent me over the edge. She cried out her own release seconds later and collapsed between my legs.

"Fuck, how is it always so good with you?" she sighed from where she fell.

I sat up and righted her so she was lying next to me. She flopped her head lazily to the side to look at me. "Nope, you gotta go, Brando."

"Jesus, Lexi. Can you give a guy a minute?" I asked, instantly agitated. I understood that this was just sex for her and that she didn't want me to stay, *but fuck*, I didn't know how much more of this *'fuck and run'* shit I could really take. Even though she didn't want more, I didn't want it to be just about sex either. Was I setting myself up for disappointment and potential heartbreak? Probably. *Okay, definitely.*

"I think I was pretty clear about the rules," Lexi started.

"Yeah, I got it," I said, and got up, gathered my clothes, and went into the bathroom. I closed the door a little harder than I had intended, but I thought maybe she'd get the hint. I was annoyed. *I wasn't built for this kind of sex only relationship with her.* After splashing some cold water on my face and dressing, I reemerged from the bathroom to find Lexi in her robe standing in the hall, arms crossed over her chest.

"What the fuck, Brandon?" she questioned. "I thought we agreed on what this was."

"We did, but maybe I'm not cut out for this, Lexi. I like—"

She held up a hand. "Let me stop you right there. Unless your next words are *'I like fucking your brains out,'* then I don't want to hear it."

"Oh, fuck this." I stormed off to the living room, grabbing my coat and shoes. Not bothering to put them on, I left her apartment, slamming the door as I did. Not my finest moment, but this girl had me so fucked up.

This was new territory for me, and I didn't know what to do. I thought I could keep my feelings out of it, but with each moment I spent with her, I knew that wasn't possible. I wanted Lexi in every way. She made it crystal clear she wasn't interested in more, yet I was falling for her, despite my better judgment and best efforts. All of her broken parts intrigued me. I wanted to tear down her walls and find out why she was so adamantly opposed to letting me in. I wanted to help her heal from whatever or whoever broke her heart.

19

LEXI

I let out a frustrated scream as the door slammed shut. *Fuck!* Brandon was ruining this. *Why couldn't he be like every other fucking guy on the planet?* It was times like this when I needed my bestie, but I couldn't tell Daphne about this situation without flat-out lying about who it was about. *Fuck it.* Since I was apparently such an asshole, I'd might as well burn all my bridges.

Daphne picked up after a few rings. "Hey, slut," she answered the phone in her usual joking fashion. Ordinarily, that wouldn't bother me, but I wasn't in the joking mood, and that particular term of endearment wasn't hitting the same.

A single fat tear slid down my cheek.

I sobbed, "Can you talk?"

"Oh, fuck. I'm coming over." I heard shuffling on the other end, followed by the jingle of car keys. "Nathan, I'm going to Lexi's," she said in a muffled tone.

"I'll drive you. The weather is pretty bad." I heard Nathan say to her. "What's wrong?"

"Babe, I'll be there soon, okay?" Daphne assured me.

"I'm okay, really. We can talk on the phone. I don't want you to have to come out in this shit weather," I lied. That was all I wanted, really. I wanted her with me, and to tell her everything. I knew I wouldn't be able to, but it didn't change the fact that I wanted to.

"Too late. Nathan and I are walking out of the apartment now. I'll be there soon."

Fifteen minutes later, Daphne was in my apartment on the couch with a glass of wine in hand. Nathan had dropped her off and left us alone for some much-needed bestie time. Thankfully, I had gotten my shit mostly together by that point and was more in control of my emotions.

"What's going on? Talk to me." Daphne sipped her wine and sat facing me on the couch with her legs crossed.

"So, I'm fucking this guy," I started. "Seeing him? I don't fucking know." Frustrated, I took a long drink from my glass while Daphne patiently waited for me to continue. "Okay, so I fucked this guy, and we agreed to make it a regular thing, because it was that good. But he's not like me. I think he wants more, and I can't give him that."

She eyed me suspiciously. "So, what's the problem? Why were *you* crying?"

"I don't know."

"Bullshit. Something happened." *Why did I call her again?* The last thing I wanted was to be called out on my bullshit, but there we were. Daphne knew me better than anyone, and she was always good at cutting through my crap.

"We got into a little tiff earlier. He had fucked my brains out, or maybe I fucked his out. Whatever. Doesn't matter. The point is, when he tried to lie down in the bed next to me, I reminded him of our rules and he got all pissy and left," I explained.

"Okay… but why were *you* upset?" Daphne continued to dig.

"Fuck if I know. I don't want to lose a good lay?" I didn't even believe myself.

"Lexi, I think you like this guy and that scares you," Daphne said very matter-of-factly. *Rude.*

"Nope. There's no way. I mean, I obviously don't hate him, but I don't want to date him either. You know I don't do relationships."

"But why?" Daphne paused to let me answer, but I busied myself by drinking more wine. She continued, "Lexi, you don't let people in. Why is that?"

I knew exactly why, but I wasn't ready to talk about it with anyone, not even her. I shook my head. "Nope, I'm not doing this."

"Don't bite my head off, but I think the reason you don't let people in is because you're afraid of getting hurt."

Fucking Daphne. She didn't know everything, but she knew enough to realize I was scared. She was hitting a little too close to home, so I tried to change the subject. "I'm fine, really. How are things with Nate Dog?"

"Don't change the subject, Lexi. I'm being serious right

now. What are you so afraid of? What happened?" She wasn't letting this go, and I was getting more and more frustrated.

I hung my head and toyed with the wineglass in my hands. "He'll just leave too," I whispered.

"Who?"

"Anyone. Men. You." I looked up at her with tears building in my eyes. I couldn't believe I was about to let her in even more than I already had. "After my dad left, my mom would cry at night when she thought I was asleep. I won't let a man do that to me. It's easier to keep people at arm's length than to be hurt when they leave."

"Oh, Lexi!" Daphne grabbed my wine, set it on the coffee table alongside hers, and pulled me into a tight hug.

Fuck, this did not go how I thought it would. But what did I think was going to happen when she came over? Why did I call her in the first place? To vent? To get validation? I didn't even know. A sob escaped me, and Daphne held me tighter.

"I'm not going anywhere, babe. You couldn't get rid of me if you tried." I tried to pull away, but Daphne held fast. "You are loved, and you deserve to be loved. I know you think not letting people in will protect your heart, but that's clearly not working for you."

"I'm fiiiiine," I said as I tried to extricate myself from her embrace.

"You are clearly not fine. I think you're doing more harm than good with the way you keep people away. Maybe you think you aren't worthy of being loved, or maybe you have serious trust issues because of your dad, but when the right guy does come along, I hope you give him a chance to prove you wrong."

"Okay, bitch, that's enough therapy for one night," I joked.

She grabbed my hands and looked me dead in the eye. "I'm serious. You deserve more than you're allowing yourself to have. I hope you see that someday."

THE NEXT DAY, I was feeling pretty shitty about the way Brandon and I had left things, so I shot him a text.

ME

Hey, I'm really sorry about last night.

He left me on read, but I didn't message him again. If he was catching feelings, I didn't want to make things any worse than they already were.

20

BRANDON

I hadn't talked to Lexi for a few days. When she texted me her apology, I wasn't ready to respond. I needed time to cool off, and I had hoped that giving her some space would be good for her, too.

I opened our text thread.

LEXI

Hey, I'm really sorry about last night.

I sat staring at the message. I knew I wanted to respond, but I didn't know what to say. *Did I want to continue with our current arrangement? Could I separate my feelings for her from the sex?*

Dylan came and sat on my station. "Hey, whatcha doing?"

I closed my messages app and put my phone down. "Nothing, waiting for my next appointment. You?"

"My appointment canceled. No one wants to go out in this weather. I hate the snow," Dylan complained.

"Aw, come on, man, it's not that bad. I mean, aside from business slowing down some. It's beautiful. It makes the city seem so peaceful."

"Peaceful? People drive like fucking assholes in this shit." He continued, "and I can't remember what it feels like to be warm."

I laughed, "Dramatic much? You've got the heat in here set to like eighty-five degrees."

"It's set at seventy-five, thank you very much. Anyway, I'm cutting out of here early. Coco was meowing at me on the kitty cam. I think she needs some extra snuggles today."

"You and that fucking cat." I shook my head and let out a laugh.

"Hey, Coco Baby is an angel and deserves all the snuggles." Dylan hopped off my station and slapped me on the back. "Have a good night, bro. Be careful getting home later."

"Will do. You too, even though you only have like a block to go." Dylan was lucky enough to find an apartment down the street from the shop. It was in the heart of everything—perfect for a young single guy in the city. My place wasn't too much farther away, but it was far enough that I usually drove when the weather was bad. I loved the snow, but not enough to risk losing toes to frostbite.

Dylan laughed. "See ya tomorrow."

I reopened my text thread with Lexi.

ME

Hey, sorry I didn't respond the other day. It's okay. You were very clear about what this was between us. I'm sorry I overreacted. I'm just not used to fucking without feelings getting involved. I'll try to keep my shit together. Promise.

I wasn't sure if I'd be able to keep my feelings out of it, but I was going to give it another try. I just wanted to be around her, in whatever capacity she'd allow. Maybe she'd soften to the idea of me in time. And if not, I was definitely headed for heartbreak, but I'd have to deal with that later. My phone dinged with an incoming message.

LEXI

I'll try not to be such a bitch and let you catch your breath before I throw you out next time. I'm not used to fucking a guy who has feelings. 😁

LEXI

Sorry again.

ME

No need to apologize, really. I gotta run. My next appointment is here. You working tomorrow? I'll be there in the afternoon for a few hours, playing Santa. 🎅

LEXI

Yeah, I'll be there. Maybe I'll stop by if it's not too busy.

I put my phone away and greeted my next client with thoughts of Lexi running through my mind.

THE NEXT DAY, while I was getting ready for my Santa shift at the hospital, I couldn't stop thinking about Lexi. I should have pushed her more—gotten to the bottom of why she was so against relationships, because I didn't merely want to fuck her. I wanted to date her, but I didn't press the issue. Didn't even bring it up. And why not? Because I was a pussy. *That's why.* I'd rather see her in secret as a fuck buddy than not see her at all. She didn't seem like the type to stick around and figure shit out. She seemed like a runner.

Damn, the parallels between this and what happened with Nathan and Daphne were crazy. The only difference— Lexi wasn't fresh out of a relationship. She was utterly against them. *Period.* Oh, and we were sneaking around like teenagers. Why Daphne and Nathan couldn't know about us escaped me. I knew Lexi had promised Daphne, but why was Daphne so against it, anyway? We were both consenting adults. Was she afraid our dating would be weird because they had just started dating? Whatever the reason, I wanted more, but was settling for sex, which was so unlike me. I hoped I'd be able to keep this up until I could figure Lexi out and break down her walls.

When I arrived at the hospital, I did my best to shake off my thoughts of Lexi. I needed to be present for the kids. Rounding on the floors was the hardest part of this volunteer gig—that was where I'd come into contact with the sickest kids. The pediatrics floor was usually more fun and lighthearted, but as I moved into the pediatric ICU and oncology floor, things always felt a little heavier. Despite that, I maintained my jolly Santa persona, hoping I'd brighten an otherwise bad day for at least some of these kids. If I could elicit even one smile from each kid, I felt like the day was a success.

After making my rounds, I went to the cafeteria to finish my shift. There, I saw kids who were visiting loved ones who were in the hospital. It was a little easier to stomach for me, although it hit a little closer to home. I wasn't believing-in-Santa age when my mom died, but spending countless hours in the hospital while she was getting treatments took its toll on me, nonetheless. That's actually how I ended up volunteering as Santa. I'd see all the kids during Christmastime in the cafeteria, visiting the jolly guy, smiling at a time that may have been the worst of their lives. When my mom died, and after I started feeling more like myself again, I wanted to do something, anything, to give back— something that she would have been proud of. Christmas was always her favorite, and it just felt right.

The kid on my lap beamed up at me as he told me all about the new video game system he wanted for Christmas.

21

LEXI

Work was trash. We were busy again and had several people call out, which meant that what should have been a cush assignment was doubled. *Un-fucking-believable.* I spent the morning changing out IV lines, updating family members, dealing with a code brown, and titrating drips. All normal ICU stuff, but when you've got two vented patients who need your attention equally, it can be a lot. It also meant breaks were short and hard to come by.

'Tis the season, I guess. By the time we got some relief, it was midafternoon, and I was desperate for a caffeine boost. I made my way to the cafeteria to grab myself a soda —certainly not to catch a glimpse of a certain sexy Santa. Did I want to see Brandon? Yes. Did I have time for a quickie? No, but for some reason, the thought of seeing him excited me anyway. I didn't know what was wrong with me. Brandon had me all sorts of fucked up.

Entering the cafeteria, I spotted him immediately, sitting in the North Pole setup with a little kid on his lap. *Oof, my ovaries!* I didn't even want kids, but damn.

I eyed him as I crossed the room toward the vending machines. He was laughing and smiling, completely oblivious that I was staring at him. While focused on him, I smacked right into someone, causing them to drop their tray of food. A crash rang out throughout the room. Heads turned, and a few assholes even clapped. But what absolutely sent me was the fact that Brandon had looked up and smirked at me before I could even turn my head to assess the damage I'd caused. *Motherfucker caught me ogling his ass.*

I quickly crouched down to help the poor guy whose lunch I'd ruined. "Oh my God, I'm so sorry," I apologized as I picked up a rogue apple.

"Lacey?"

I looked up to see someone who looked somewhat familiar. I squinted my eyes. He sort of resembled what's-his-name that I hooked up with last month. "Oh, hey. It's Lexi, actually," I said as he crouched down to my level.

What's-his-name and I put the rest of the mess onto his tray and then stood up as a janitor approached with a mop. "Thank you so much. Sorry for the mess," I said to him, and then turned back to what's-his-name.

"I'm so sorry about that. I wasn't looking where I was going. Let me buy you a new lunch," I offered.

"No, really. It's okay. But you could let me take you out to dinner, though. To make it up to you for blowing you off last month," he chuckled nervously and grabbed the back of his neck.

"You blew *me* off? Sorry to say, but the feeling was mutual," I laughed. Just then, I clocked Brandon in my peripheral vision. I wasn't sure how to play this. I could use good old what's-his-name again and make Brando jealous, or I could be a normal, well-adjusted-grown-up.

"I'd never done anything like that before." He leaned in closer and said in a hushed voice, "You know, had a one-night stand. I was sort of going through something, and I feel like I kind of used you. I feel terrible about it, and I'm really sorry." He seemed genuine, and a strange feeling came over me. *Was that guilt? Did I actually feel bad for using him?*

I reached out and touched his arm as Brandon reached us. "Everything okay here, Lexi?" I dropped my hand from the guy's arm like it was lava. Brandon towered over us, and he appeared to puff himself up so that he was somehow even larger than usual. *Fucking men. Insert dramatic eye roll here.*

"Yeah. Everything's fine." I directed my attention back to the guy. "I wasn't paying attention. Sorry again—" I trailed off, still unsure of the guy's name.

"Mark," he smiled. "So how about dinner?"

Brandon's eyes flashed with something akin to anger before he grabbed my arm to pull me away. "She's already got plans tonight, Matt," he shot over his shoulder.

"What the fuck, Brandon?" I barked, keeping my voice low. Moments later, I was being pushed into an on-call room. "What is your fucking problem?" I whisper yelled.

The door slammed, and Brandon was on me. With his hand on my throat, he pushed me against the wall. He was rough yet gentle, clearly not trying to hurt me, but definitely staking his claim. My pussy clenched at nothing. *Traitorous whore.*

"Who was that guy? You know him." It wasn't a question.

"He's no one." I tried to push him away, but it was like trying to push an elephant. "And what business is it of yours, anyway?"

"Who is he?"

"Jesus, you're such a Neanderthal. He's just a guy I fucked once, okay? Can I go back to work now?" I huffed.

"When?" Brandon's eyes narrowed, and he leaned in close. *Fuck, I was so turned on.*

"Before you," I breathed. "There's been no one since we started seeing each other." *Seeing each other? What the fuck, Lexi?* And why was I telling him any of this? It wasn't his fucking business what I did or with whom.

"Good girl," he hissed. "You're mine, Sweetheart." His other hand moved between my legs. "This is mine."

Yep, that did it. I was soaked. Despite really having to get back to work, I ground myself into his touch.

"Tell me." Brandon's breath danced along my neck, sending a shiver down my body. "Whose pussy is this, Lexi?"

"Yours," I replied breathlessly.

"And the rest of you?"

"Yours." Never have I ever, in all of my years of fucking dudes, said that to anyone.

Not for fun.

Not in the heat of the moment.

Not for anything.

Yet there I was, giving myself to this man, and I think I may have actually believed what I was saying.

"Good girl." He released me and backed away. "Now get back to work. I'll be seeing you later." And then he was gone, and I was left standing there completely dumbfounded and sopping wet. *What the fuck just happened?* A frustrated growl escaped me. I didn't even have time to grab a soda.

22

BRANDON

Seeing Lexi with that guy in the cafeteria shouldn't have set me off, but it did. When she touched his arm and he asked her out, it made me want to throw her over my shoulder and storm out of the hospital with her. I was actually surprised that I didn't drop that guy. Although it wasn't his really fault. It was mine. This thing with Lexi had started as one thing but had developed into something else altogether. Well, at least for me it had. Despite what she said in that on-call room, I knew better. She wasn't mine. *Yet.*

ME

> Come over after work. We've got some
> unfinished business.

It felt so weird to text that, even though I was trying to play it cool. I didn't want whatever this was. I wanted more.

LEXI

We'll see.

She was infuriating. So aloof. So unlike anyone I'd ever been with.

ME

We'll see? I don't think so, Sweetheart. I will see you later. You can either come to my place after work, or I'll show up at yours. It's your choice.

Text bubbles appeared and disappeared. She was probably deciding whether or not to be a smart ass.

LEXI

Fine.

ME

Good girl.

23

———

LEXI

Christmas Eve

I woke up feeling great. Things with Brandon had been going so well. The sex was straight fire, and he wasn't pressuring me for more. I spent the past week being less of a bitch, and Brandon hadn't overstayed his welcome. It was a perfect situation.

I excitedly got ready for the day. First up was my tattoo session with him, and then I planned to spend the day with him and his family. Ordinarily, I'd be freaking the fuck out, but it was Daphne who invited me, and she'd be there as a buffer.

I arrived at the shop a few minutes before my appointment and tapped on the door to let Brandon know I was there. He had let me know that the shop would technically be closed and to knock when I arrived. A gust of wind blew some flurries into my face. I shivered and pulled my collar up as I waited for him to open the door. Dressed for the day in fleece-lined leggings and an oversized sweater with a fluffy down-filled jacket that went to my knees and a hat and gloves, I should have been warm enough. I was not. *Fuck this weather.*

The door to the shop opened, and I pushed past Brandon to get out of the cold. I was pleasantly surprised to find the shop warmer than expected.

"Fuck, it's so cold out there today," I said as I stomped my boots on the mat to remove some of the snow I was tracking in.

"Yeah, no kidding. It was freezing in here when I got in."

"When did you get here?" I asked.

"About an hour ago. I wanted to get here early and get the heat on for you. I figured it'd be cold this morning," he explained. "Can I take your coat?"

I nodded, allowing him to help me out of my coat. "Well, my cold bones appreciate that. Especially since I'm about to be half naked," I chuckled.

Brandon paused behind me, his breath on my neck. "I can't wait." And then he was gone, depositing my coat on the coat tree by the entry. *Fuck, the effect this man had on me.* I already wanted to jump his bones, but that wasn't why I was there. We had work to do before heading to his dad's later that day.

"Behave," I joked. "This leg isn't going to tattoo itself."

He held his hand up with two fingers. "I'll be on my very best behavior. Scout's honor."

"Ha! You probably *were* a Boy Scout, huh?"

"I was not actually, but thanks for the compliment?" He started walking towards his station. "Come on, Sweetheart. Let's get some color on that octopus."

His station was already set up and ready, so we got right to it. Not bothering to wait for him to go out from behind the privacy screen, I kicked off my shoes and stripped out of my leggings and thong. I'd never been shy about my body, so why start then? He'd already seen all of me after all.

Brandon cleared his throat, drawing my attention. "What? It's not like you haven't seen all of *this*," I said, motioning to my crotch area.

His eyes burned into mine. "That doesn't mean I'm unaffected by the sight of you, Lexi. And if you want your tattoo finished this century, I suggest you cover up." He threw a sheet at me and then stalked off into the back room.

He was cute when he was trying to keep it together, but I covered up and got into position on the table. I really wanted this tattoo finished, and I was willing to behave to make that happen.

Brandon returned a few moments later. "Ready?"

"Ready."

WE MADE some really significant progress on my tattoo. One more session and it would probably be done. I'd miss spending time with Brandon like that, though. He was comfortable to be around, although it was a little weird for me to be spending time with a guy with our clothes on. But things weren't awkward or weird, and conversation flowed freely. Maybe I was growing more open to the idea of letting him in?

After we had finished with my tattoo for the day, Brandon suggested we check out the Christmas market a few streets over. He said he still needed to grab something for his dad, and I hoped I could find some last-minute things for my mom, who was impossible to shop for. If she wanted something, she'd buy it, so asking her what she wanted for Christmas was always a lost cause.

Bundled up in our winter gear, we exited the shop, where soft flurries falling from the sky greeted us. I pulled my hat down over my ears and tugged my collar up a little higher, thankful that the wind wasn't blowing. It was still cold, but with only a couple of blocks to the market, it definitely could have been worse. I hated the snow, but turning to look at Brandon, I could tell he loved this shit. He was grinning like an idiot, and I swore I saw him stick his tongue out to catch a snowflake. *What a lunatic.*

The Christmas market had vendors of all kinds—most were local businesses. The enticing smells from the various food vendors made my stomach growl, but I was holding out for whatever Brandon's dad had in store for us. We moved from vendor to vendor, holding up items we thought were cute or funny for the other to see. We laughed and joked. It was nice.

Brandon motioned to a food vendor and asked, "Did you want a hot chocolate or something?"

"Sure. That sounds great, actually. I'm freezing."

"Okay, I'll be right back," he said and then gave me an unexpected peck that warmed my cool cheek before walking away. I looked after him in shock. That was definitely not a friend or fuck buddy kind of thing to do. I brushed away my thoughts to concentrate on finding something for my mom or a gift for Brandon's dad.

I came across a leather-bound sketchbook I thought would be a perfect gift for Brandon, but stopped myself. We were *not* giving each other gifts.

Just then, Brandon returned with our hot chocolates. "Find something?" he asked.

"Maybe. You think your dad would like this?"

"That's really sweet, but you don't have to get him anything," Brandon answered.

"I can't show up empty-handed. That's rude." I protested.

"Well, if you insist on bringing something, I think that's a great gift. He'd love it, actually, and he'd definitely use it."

"Okay, I'll take it," I said, turning my attention toward the vendor.

Brandon and I continued through the market, warmer with our hot chocolates in hand. Fat snowflakes fell slowly all around us, and live music played throughout the square —it almost felt as if we were a normal couple out on a date. I shook the idea from my mind as we passed where the musicians were performing. My attention was focused on the performance until Brandon swept me up in his arms and started dancing with me. Or I should say, attempted to dance with me. I was frozen in place.

He leaned down, his mouth grazing my ear. "Relax, Sweetheart. Just go with it."

Fuck it, I thought. *What's the harm in having a little fun today? I can go back to being my hard-ass self tomorrow.*

My body moved in time with his, keeping pace with the music. Other couples joined us on the makeshift dance floor in the middle of the city street. Snow continued to fall, and I allowed myself to relax into Brandon's arms, but I was looking anywhere but at him. Looking into his eyes would be too much. I could feel my chest tightening.

"Hey, you okay?" Brandon asked, sounding worried. I plastered on a smile and looked up at him.

What.

A.

Fucking.

Mistake.

The concerned look on his face gave way to a huge grin as soon as my eyes met his. My smile, which started as a lie, grew, and I knew in that moment that I was in trouble. *Fuck.*

24

———

BRANDON

Looking down at Lexi and seeing her like this cracked my heart wide open. *Maybe she was softening toward me. Maybe this could work.* I leaned in to kiss her as she seemed to come to her senses, her eyes wide. She pushed her hands against my chest.

"Brandon, don't."

Fuck me. Right when I thought she was letting her guard down, she went back on high alert. I shouldn't have pushed my luck. Going in for a kiss at that moment was too much, and she was shutting me out. *Again.*

I stepped back and pulled at the back of my neck. "Lex, I'm sorry, it's just—"

Her hand shot up. "It's fine, really. Let's just go, okay?" She turned and walked off.

I hung my head for a breath, defeated, but quickly shook it off and followed her back toward the shop and my car.

WE ARRIVED at my dad's place about thirty minutes later. The drive wasn't awkward or quiet. In fact, Lexi didn't seem affected by what had transpired at all. I appeared to be the only one freaking the fuck out. Thankfully, I kept my spiraling thoughts to myself as I attempted to show no outward signs of my internal turmoil.

My dad's place was all decked out. It was always Mom's favorite holiday, and she made Dad get up on a ladder each year to put up lights—a tradition he'd continued since her passing.

"Wow. This looks great," Lexi commented as we walked up the few stairs to the front door.

"Yeah, Dad always goes all out." I opened the door and guided Lexi inside.

"Hello?" my dad called from the kitchen.

"It's me and Lexi," I replied as I helped her out of her coat.

Daphne, Nathan, and my dad rounded the corner from the kitchen to greet us. Everyone took turns hugging one another. Lexi tried to shake my dad's hand, but he pulled her into one of his famous bear hugs. He wasn't really the hand-shake type.

She handed him the sketchbook she'd gotten him at the market as we started towards the kitchen. "Lexi, this was very thoughtful. I love it, but you didn't have to bring anything."

"My mom always taught me not to show up empty-handed, and I thought you could use this for your art," Lexi replied.

"Sounds like your mom did a great job with you," Dad said as we reached the kitchen.

Dad didn't host a fancy sit down dinner like Mom would've. That wasn't his style, but the food looked and smelled amazing, and was set up buffet-style in the kitchen.

"Did Nathan help you with all of this, pops?" I asked.

"And Daphne. They've been here most of the day helping me get ready," Dad answered while pulling Daphne in for a side hug.

Daphne animatedly shook her head. "Oh, no. This was all you guys. I was solely here for moral support and to taste test the wine," Daphne joked. "Speaking of wine—Lexi?"

"You don't have to twist my arm," Lexi answered.

The front door opened, and moments later Dylan walked in with his cat, Coco, in tow—decked out in her Christmas best. *I'm not kidding.* This cat came prancing in on a freaking leash, wearing a plaid jacket with her head held high. *I'm not exaggerating when I say that that cat was spoiled with a capital S.*

A squeal cut through the air. I turned to see Lexi with her hands on her cheeks and the ungodly noise emanating from her. She ran and dropped to the floor in front of Coco, who began aggressively rubbing herself all over her.

"Oh, isn't she the sweetest?" Lexi cooed. "What's her name?"

My brother beamed proudly. "This is Coco Baby."

Lexi plopped back onto her butt and allowed Coco to climb into her arms. "Who's the prettiest baby? You are. Aren't you? Oh, my God. You're so sweet."

This continued for several minutes until my dad cleared his throat. "If you're done fawning over my grandkitty, dinner's just about ready."

Lexi looked up, her cheeks reddened. "Oh, shit. I'm sorry. But seriously, has there ever been a prettier cat?"

"No, there hasn't. She's definitely the prettiest," Dylan chimed in proudly and then offered his hand to Lexi. As her hand slipped into his, a pang of jealousy shot through me. I couldn't remember a time before Lexi when I'd ever felt jealousy. Now every time another man even looked at her, I felt it. But this was my brother, and I had no reason to be jealous. Lexi and I weren't even a thing.

"Now that everyone's here, let's eat," Dad said as he clapped his hands together.

We filled our plates and then gathered in the dining room to eat. The table looked like Mom had set it, complete with her favorite Christmas tablecloth and centerpiece decorations. There were even candles lit, which I attributed to Daphne's presence this year. Dad still decorated for Christmas, but didn't keep up with all the details Mom would have.

"This all looks great," I mentioned as I took my seat and, through no scheming on my part, Lexi and I ended up sitting next to one another. The table fell into easy conversation. It was awesome having Daphne and Lexi here to celebrate with us this year. The holidays with my brothers and dad were nice, but since Mom's death, there was an underlying sadness to our celebrations. This year seemed different with the ladies present—*lighter even.* I was obviously still sad Mom wasn't with us, but hearing Lexi's laugh throughout dinner seemed to ease the pain in my chest.

Lexi moaned next to me, drawing my attention. "Oh, my God! This is soooo good. Who made these mashed potatoes?" she asked.

"Nathan and Daphne did," my dad answered her. "The only thing I'm taking credit for this year is the turkey. I deep-fried it this time, and it turned out pretty good, if I do say so myself."

Lexi continued to moan, "It's soooo juicy. Like seriously, I've never had turkey this moist before." I choked a little on my drink and began coughing.

"You okay there, Brando?" Lexi turned toward me, looking not at all concerned.

I couldn't seem to stop coughing, but I attempted to talk in between fits. "Just—*cough*—went down—*cough*—the wrong—*cough*—pipe."

"I remember my first drink," Dad joked, and everyone around the table snickered.

"Thanks—*cough*—for nothing, Dad—*cough cough*." Tears built in my eyes as another fit of coughing overcame me. It must have been at least a full minute more before I finally stopped coughing, and conversations started back up around the table.

Lexi leaned over towards me slightly and whispered, "All that because I said the word *moist*?"

Cough. Fucking Lexi. "You'll pay for this," I promised under my breath as I grabbed her upper thigh under the cover of the tablecloth.

"Mmmhmm." She smiled coyly and went back to eating her meal, ignoring my touch. Then, I glanced at Dylan, who was staring at me with a smirk. *Busted.* There was no way he didn't catch that little back and forth. I quickly scanned the rest of the table, but everyone else was engaged in conversations.

I managed to make it through dinner without choking to death, so I considered that a win. After everyone had finished, I started clearing the plates. If you cooked in this house, you didn't clean, so I already knew I was in for some dish duty.

"I'll help," Lexi said as she stood from the table. *Well, that was unexpected.* I'd assumed that once we entered my dad's that she'd avoid me like the plague, but there she was offering to help me with the dishes.

In the kitchen, we stood shoulder to shoulder at the sink. I washed, and she dried. "Are you sure it's safe for us to be in here together?" I whispered. "Aren't you worried Daphne will suspect something?"

"I may have to tell her soon," Lexi said, and then chewed her lip. I almost dropped the dish that was in my hand.

"And what prompted this change of heart?" I asked.

"It has nothing to do with my heart. She's my best friend, and I feel like an asshole for lying to her. I really didn't think we'd still be going at it."

"What's going on in here?" Dylan said loudly as he walked into the kitchen, startling me. The dish I was washing slipped through my soapy fingers with a crash.

"Shit!" I quickly scrambled to pick up the dish. Thankfully, it hadn't broken.

"Jumpy much, bro?" Dylan laughed. "Hey Lexi, you're a guest. You don't have to do the dishes. I can't believe this rude asshole roped you into dish duty. Why don't you join the others in the back room? I bet Coco Baby would love some snuggles by the fire."

Lexi looked up at me in question. We really needed to finish our conversation, but it wasn't the place or the time. "Go, Dylan and I've got this," I assured her. She nodded and strutted off to join the others. I couldn't help but watch her as she went, hips swaying all the way.

Dylan took Lexi's spot next to me and nodded in her direction. "So, what's going on there?"

Well, shit. "Nothing, why?" I replied almost too quickly.

Dylan laughed. "Holy shit! You're fucking her!" Thankfully, he kept his voice low enough so I didn't think anyone else heard him.

"Shhh. Jeez, Dylan," I scolded. "She doesn't want anyone to know."

"Ooooo, so you're her dirty little secret. Hot! But very unlike you." Dylan placed his hand on his chest. "I'm so proud."

"Oh, fuck off. It's not like that. I really like her."

"Does she know that?"

"No. I don't know. Maybe. It doesn't matter. She's not

interested in more than what we're doing, so I'm trying to keep things casual." I let out an exasperated sigh. "But I don't know how much longer I can keep this up."

"You aren't cut out for my no-strings-attached lifestyle, my friend," Dylan chuckled. "Wait, why doesn't she want anyone to know? Who cares if you guys are hooking up?"

"I don't know. She made some promise to Daphne about not fucking me," I relayed, shaking my head. I still didn't understand the whole situation. *I mean, why should it even matter who Lexi slept with?*

Dylan sputtered, "What the fuck? I'm so confused."

"You and me both, brother. But it doesn't really matter. Lexi doesn't want a relationship, anyway." I shook my head and passed Dylan a plate. "But you're right. I'm not cut out for this casual shit. I want more."

"See, that's your fatal flaw. You and Nathan both, actually. You let your heart lead you, whereas I let something else lead me." He waggled his eyebrows, resembling Groucho Marx. "If you know what I mean?"

"Unfortunately, I *do* know what you mean," I laughed.

25

LEXI

The back room was the perfect after-dinner hangout spot. It was so warm and cozy, complete with a roaring fire and plenty of comfortable seating. Through the large windows, a light dusting of snow fell gently, creating a peaceful backdrop. Nathan and Daphne were all snuggled up on a loveseat. *Bleck.* Mr. Pierce, Dane as he insisted I call him, was in his leather recliner, leaving another recliner and a larger couch open when I entered the room. Coco was lying on the floor by the fire on her back, looking as happy as a clam. I didn't want to disturb her, so I sat on the couch. I settled in and pulled a blanket up over my legs. To my surprise, Coco immediately hopped up and curled up on my lap, purring loudly. *Damn, she was cute.*

"So, how's the tattoo coming along, Lexi?" Nathan asked. "Brandon said you had one more session to go?"

"Yeah, it's going great. I really love what he did, and I'm excited to see it all finished." It really was looking good. Brandon was so talented. *And funny. And charming. And sexy as hell. And could fuck like a god. Bitch, get your shit together,* I thought. I did not need to be thinking any of those things about Brandon. He was just a guy I was fucking, nothing more. Although that wasn't really true anymore, and I knew it. Lying to myself was getting harder by the day. But what was I going to do, let him in? Brandon seemed like a nice enough guy, but he didn't really want to date me. Maybe he thought he wanted that, but I knew better, and I'd be damned if I let him in only for him to leave me, too.

Meow. Coco interrupted my thoughts, pushing her head into my hand. I must have stopped petting her, and she wasn't shy about voicing her disapproval. I resumed showering her with attention as Dylan and Brandon rejoined the party. Dylan, entering ahead of Brandon, took a seat on the couch next to me, forcing Brandon onto the remaining recliner. He eyed me, and then his gaze shifted to Dylan, who was now leaning over to give his cat some of his attention.

"She really likes you, Lexi," Dylan said with a wink, catching me off guard. *What the fuck?* Don't get me wrong, Dylan was also very good-looking, but he wasn't my type at all. I chalked his flirty look up to him being in a perpetual state of flirting—according to Daphne, he was a fuckboy, after all.

It was then that I made the mistake of looking back in Brandon's direction. *Big mistake.* The fire burning behind his glare was like an electric shock straight to my pussy. It was the same look he'd given me in the bar when I was trying to get a rise out of him. He was jealous. I arched an eyebrow at him. Knowing I'd pay for it later—*hopefully with orgasms*—I doubled down, 'accidentally' brushing Dylan's hand with mine as I pet the adorable fluff ball in my lap, while looking directly into Brandon's eyes. His nostrils flared as he slowly—*almost imperceivably*—shook his head.

My barely there smile tugged at the edges of my mouth. *It was so on, motherfucker.* I hadn't had this much fun with a guy in forever, and I wanted to draw this out as long as possible. Whatever *this* was. *Would I break his heart? Would he break mine?* Signs pointed to yes on both accounts, but I didn't give a single solitary fuck at that moment.

Daphne laughed at something Nathan was saying from her place nestled at his side. *Good.* That meant she wasn't paying any attention to Brandon and my little back and forth, but Dylan saw it. He eyed me with a grin hidden from the others, from where he was now lying on the couch with his head by Coco.

I had to talk to Daphne. There was no way this was staying under wraps for much longer, and if Brandon and I were going to keep this up, I'd rather she hear it from me first. As soon as we had our next girls' night, I'd confess, but until then, I needed to be more careful.

THE REST of the evening was absolutely lovely. Brandon's family made me feel right at home, which was nice since I was missing celebrating with my mom this year. After we said our goodbyes and were safely inside Brandon's car, away from prying eyes, he turned to me with a look I couldn't quite place.

"What?" I asked innocently.

He raised an eyebrow and leaned into my space. I glanced back towards the house and pushed him back. "Stop it. Not here."

"Oh, *now* you're worried about getting caught? What about all of that flirting you were doing with my brother for my benefit?"

"I was *not* flirting with your brother." *Okay, I was flirting a little*, but it was only to annoy him. And from the look that was plastered on his face earlier and the look he was giving me then, it had worked.

"Liar. You were trying to make me jealous, and you know it." He put his arm over the back of my seat to look behind us as he reversed the car. His scent washed over me, and I almost leaned into it—into him. *Almost.*

I sat up straighter in my seat, trying to stay focused. "Why would I try to make you jealous? And with your brother?" I scoffed.

"Really? It's not the first time you've intentionally tried to get a reaction from me by flirting with someone else, Lexi." He side-eyed me as we drove down the lightly snow-covered road.

I rolled my eyes. "I did no such thing."

We stopped at the end of the street; he gripped my thigh roughly, causing me to audibly gasp. "Look at me." My eyes shot to his. His nostrils flared. "You. Are. Mine." He ground out each word like it physically hurt him.

I started to protest, but swallowed my words when Brandon pulled me into a frantic kiss. "I've wanted to do this all night." His muffled words escaped between kisses.

I pushed against his chest. "Brandon," his name came out breathy and desperate, more like a plea than a protest.

With his hand on the back of my neck, he rested his forehead on mine. "Dammit, Lexi. I know I don't have your heart, and I know this is just sex—" the *for you* left unsaid "—but you are mine, for as long as this lasts."

Well, fuck. "Brandon, this needs to be just sex for you, too, or it's not going to work. Feelings make things messy." I sat back and focused my gaze out my window, hoping we could drop it.

Brandon let out a breath and then continued to drive us back into the city. After about ten minutes of awkward silence, I spoke without looking in his direction. "I'm going to tell Daphne."

"What's changed?"

"We're both consenting adults, and lying to her is killing me." I turned in my seat to face him. "Promising not to hook up with you was a mistake. I need to clear the air with her. I'm sure it won't be a big deal."

Brandon glanced back at me and then placed his hand on my thigh. "What are you going to tell her about us exactly?"

"I don't know. The truth, I guess—that we're hooking up sometimes?" I didn't really know how to describe Brandon and my situationship. I'd had fuck buddies before, but we didn't talk much and definitely didn't hang out outside of the bedroom. The problem with my current situation was that I actually liked Brandon, and I didn't want to hurt his feelings, which was a new development for me.

I guess I could understand why Daphne didn't want me to get involved with him. She knew I'd end up hurting him, and she was trying to protect him from her fuck-and-run friend. *If I had half a heart, I'd end things with him and spare him the inevitable heartache, but I was a heartless fuckgirl, right? So why not lean into it?*

Brandon removed his hand from my thigh and focused back on the road. "Yeah, we're hooking up sometimes."

26

BRANDON

I clenched my jaw and gripped the steering wheel a little tighter, attempting to take my frustrations out on it. *Hooking up sometimes? Is that really all this was ever going to be with her? Could I live with that?* I knew the answer. This wasn't me. I didn't want casual, but Lexi didn't want to let me in.

The rest of the drive back into the city was quiet. My thoughts continued to spiral. When I pulled up outside of Lexi's building, she turned to me with a huge grin, as if everything was fine. "You want to come up?" she asked, waggling her eyebrows at me.

"Nah, I'd better get home. It's getting late," I replied flatly.

Lexi reached out and grabbed my arm, her relaxed smile now gone. "Are we okay?"

"Yeah, we're good."

She eyed me cautiously. "Okay, I guess I'll see ya around, then." I kept my eyes focused ahead with my hands still white-knuckling the steering wheel, while she reluctantly got out of the car. "Merry Christmas, Brandon."

The door closed, and I immediately regretted how we'd left things—how I'd left things. Sure, it would have been easy to go up to her place and spend the night buried inside of her, but that would only prolong the inevitable. This wasn't going anywhere, and I needed to either get on board with that or get the fuck out.

AFTER A FITFUL NIGHT OF SLEEP, I went back to my dad's place to spend the day with him and Dylan. Christmas Day wasn't the same without Mom, but we always tried to make the best of it. Usually, we were all there, but this year we were down one, thanks to Nathan being with Daphne and her family.

"You should've just stayed here last night, son. I don't like your driving back and forth from the city in this weather," Dad scolded as we took our seats in the back room.

"I had to get Lexi home," I replied.

"Yeah, he had to '*get her home*,'" Dylan said, using air quotes. *What an ass.*

"Oh, what's this? Are you guys dating?" Dad asked.

"Jesus, Dylan." I shot Dylan a look that hopefully

conveyed how uncool he was being. "No, we aren't. I'm working on her tattoo. We're just friends."

"She seems nice, and it was really thoughtful of her to bring me that sketchbook. Whatever's going on between you two, you seem happier."

"What do you mean?" I asked.

"I'm not saying that you've been unhappy, just that you seem happier. If Lexi has something to do with that, then that's great." Dad reclined his chair back. "How about you, Dylan? Any lucky lady in your life?"

I laughed out loud. "That'll be the day."

"Yeah, no thanks, pops. Looks like Nathan is your only hope for grandkids at this point," Dylan chuckled. "Don't worry. You still have Coco Baby." Coco let out a small meow from her place by the fire. I'd swear that cat understood what we were saying.

"And I love her, but you boys need to settle down, find your person. I don't really care about grandkids; I only want you all to be happy. If you can find a love even half as good as what your mom and I had, I'd be thrilled." He stared out the window for a moment, as he sometimes did whenever he thought about Mom.

Dylan, with his uncanny ability to *not* read the room, chimed in. "Yeah, I'm good. I'm not tying myself down to one woman for the rest of my life. No, thank you. After all, they say variety is the spice of life, right?"

"I hope for your own sake that you eat your words one day, my boy," Dad chuckled.

"So how are you enjoying being back at the shop, Pops?" I asked, trying to steer the conversation back to safer topics.

"It's been great, actually. I can't believe I stayed away for so long, though." He shook his head. "Your mother would be so disappointed. She never wanted me to mourn her like that." *So much for safer topics.* "She made me promise not to, but I just couldn't go back there. Not right away anyway."

"I hope you didn't think we were pressuring you to come back," I added. "We just wanted you to get out of the house. To get back to living your life."

"I know, son, and I'm glad you guys pushed me. I needed it." He smiled at me and then turned his attention to Dylan. "Besides, someone has to keep you boys in line over there."

"Why are you looking at me?" Dylan asked, looking offended.

"Remember that day you brought Coco into the shop?"

"Oh my God, Dad. It was one time, and it was an *emergency*," Dylan huffed.

"It was not an emergency, and the last thing we need is someone shutting us down because your air conditioning broke. Coco would have been fine at home that day, and you know it."

"It was like 100 degrees!" Dylan argued.

I laughed. "You're ridiculous. You know Coco is not your actual child, right?"

"Whatever." Dylan rolled his eyes and moved to scoop Coco up from her place on the floor, nuzzling into her neck. "Don't listen to them, you sweet angel. Daddy loves you the most."

Dad and I burst into laughter as Dylan stalked off to the kitchen with Coco Baby in his arms.

27

———————

LEXI

I ended up working on Christmas Day. It was easy to pick up because hardly anyone wanted to work the holidays on our unit, even with the extra pay. Since I had nothing else to do and really didn't feel like spending the day alone in my apartment, I decided to work. Besides, I needed a distraction. I hated the way Brandon and I had left things, which was a new feeling for me. I couldn't remember ever giving a shit about a fuck buddy's feelings before. The moment I closed the door to his car, I knew he was upset, and my chest had been aching ever since. I tried to chalk it up to one too many servings of mashed potatoes, but apparently, I cared about Brandon.

Ready to celebrate a belated Christmas, I arrived at my mom's apartment the day after with Chinese takeout. It had been only the two of us for so long, and we usually spent every holiday together unless one of us was working. Mom wasn't much of a cook, what with having to work and take care of me all alone. We basically lived on frozen foods and takeout, but I never complained.

"Hey, Mom," I greeted as I walked into her kitchen, where she was sitting at the kitchen table, scrolling on her phone.

"Oh, hey Lexi bug. I didn't hear you come in," she replied, putting her phone down and rising to pull me into a powerful hug. I melted into her embrace. *God, I missed her.* Even though we talked often, we didn't see each other as much as I'd like. With her work schedule as a bartender and mine as a nurse, it was hard to find a day when neither of us had to work. I squeezed her tighter.

"Is everything okay, kiddo?" she asked, sounding a little concerned.

"Yeah, I'm fine," I replied, took a step back, and lifted the bag still in my hand. "I brought Chinese."

"Yum, my favorite. Put it on the table. I'll grab some plates." As I unpacked our food, she called over her shoulder, "So how was work yesterday?"

"Meh. It was okay. Nothing too crazy, and some family members brought us food, so that was nice."

"And Christmas Eve? Whose house did you go to again?" she asked as she set a plate down in front of me.

"Daphne's boyfriend's dad's house." My mouth watered as I dumped some lo mein onto my plate.

"And her boyfriend is Nathan?"

"Mmmhmm," I answered as I shoveled those tasty noodles into my mouth.

"And Nathan's brother is the one doing your tattoo?"

Mom loved details. She wanted to know everyone's name, who was seeing whom, and never forgot a thing.

"Yep. Brandon. His other brother also works at the shop, and their dad too."

"Ooooo, is their dad single?" Mom raised an eyebrow. "Is he hot? I love a guy with tattoos."

"Mom, gross. I'm eating here." I pretended to gag. "And what do you mean, you love a guy with tattoos? Since when?"

"Well, I *am* a grown-ass woman, last I checked. Have been for a while now," she laughed. "And I have needs, kiddo."

"Can we not, Mom, please?" This conversation was not happening. The last thing I wanted to talk about was my mom's *needs*. *Ewe*. "Wait. Seriously though, do you date? I don't remember you dating growing up."

"Well, it's not like I brought guys around you, but yes, I dated. I'm dating." *Interesting*. Here I thought my mom was still pining for my dad. "You're twenty-six, Lexi. Do you really think I haven't had sex all this time?"

"Jesus, Mom."

"What? Grow up. You weren't conceived by immaculate conception, you know." My mom was being way too casual about this conversation. Meanwhile, everything I thought I knew was unraveling at the seams.

"Mom, I'm not an idiot. I know you've had sex, but it's not something I really want to talk about." I chewed my lip. "I'm more surprised to learn that you dated when I was younger."

"I didn't bring anyone around because things never got that serious. I wasn't about to bring just anyone around my daughter."

"Yeah, that makes sense, but I guess I always thought you were too sad about Dad leaving to date." I shrugged my shoulders, not believing I was actually having this conversation with my mom after all of these years.

Mom reached across the table to grab my hand. "I was sad when your dad left, and it took me a long time to get over that, but I did get over it. We were just kids ourselves when we had you, and your dad didn't want the same life as I did. It devastated me when he left, but I know now that it was for the best."

"You never talked about him, and I never brought it up because I didn't want to make you sad," I recalled all the times I'd seen her crying when I was supposed to be in bed. How could I have possibly asked about the person who was causing her so much pain?

"And I never brought him up because I didn't want to upset you. Guess we both weren't very good at communicating. But I'm your mom, and I should have talked about him more, or at least asked you if you wanted to know about him. I'm sorry." A single tear slipped down her cheek.

I got up and pulled her into a hug. "Please don't cry… You did a great job being both my mom and my dad. I never asked because I didn't want to upset you, but also because screw him. Screw him for leaving you to do this all on your own." *Shit, now I was getting emotional.* I did my best to hide it, but several tears worked their way out and down my face, which was now buried in my mom's hair.

"I wouldn't have changed a thing, Lexi bug. You're my entire world." We stayed like that for a few moments, and then she continued, "It was for the best, believe me."

I pulled away and wiped my damn leaky eyes. "What do you mean?"

"Well, I guess you're old enough to know." She sat back and looked at her hands in her lap, searching for her next words.

"To know what, Mom?"

"Your dad ended up taking a pretty rough road. He started drinking and doing drugs, and eventually ended up in and out of jail. I kept track of him for a while, but the last I heard, he was out west somewhere." She took a deep breath. "He tried to come back once, but he was so fucked up, I couldn't let him anywhere near you. That's when we moved to the city. I didn't want him to find us again."

"Shit, Mom. I had no idea."

"How could you? You were so young—I didn't want you to think about that kind of stuff, and then, as you got older, I didn't see the point in bringing it up. I always figured you'd ask if you wanted to know."

I sat quietly, mulling over this new information. *Did this change the way I felt about my absentee father?* Not really. He still left. Knowing he chose drugs and alcohol over a relationship with me, over us, didn't change my opinion of him.

"Do you think you'll ever let someone in again?" I whispered.

"I have, several times, actually, but they weren't for me. What happened with your dad was a long time ago, and it doesn't affect me the way it did when I was younger. We were kids who thought we were in love, but I know now that's not what it was, and I'm ready for the real thing whenever it comes along."

All this time, I thought she was pining for my dad and closing herself off from love, but she was actually dating and putting herself out there.

"Aren't you afraid of getting hurt again?" I asked, needing to know the answer now more than ever.

"I guess so, but it's not going to stop me from living my life." She grabbed my hand again. "I might get hurt again, but it's a risk I'm willing to take because I'd eventually like to find my forever partner. Life can be pretty lonely without someone to share it with."

"You're lonely?" My heart ached for her.

"Sometimes. But I have great friends, and I have you. Having a partner would just be the icing on my already pretty great cake." She sat back in her chair. "I'm content with my life, Lexi. If I never find someone, that would be okay too, but if I find him, I'm going to hold on tight for as long as we have together. How's the saying go? It's better to have loved and lost?"

"I'm seeing a whole other side of you, Mom."

"You really thought I spent the last twenty-some years sitting here pining for your father?"

"I thought you were trying to avoid having your heart broken again."

"Is that what you're doing?" She asked, catching me off guard.

"What do you mean?"

"You know exactly what I mean. I don't think you've ever had a serious relationship, and you don't really let people get close, from what I've noticed." She leveled me with a serious look.

"First of all, I dated in college." *Lie*. Unless you consider a string of one-night stands as dating. "Second, Daphne and I are very close, and I have friends at work." She was touching on a very sore subject, especially now with how things were with Brandon.

"You can't spend your whole life pushing people away."

"And why not?" The question fell out of my mouth involuntarily. I should have protested—denied the accusation—but it was true, and lying to my mom didn't feel like something I wanted to do.

"Oh, Lexi. I'm sorry your dad wasn't around. I'm sorry I didn't show you a better example of healthy relationships," she sighed.

"Don't you dare blame yourself. You are the best mom I could've asked for. I love you so much." I batted the tears away that had trickled down my face.

Mom's arms wrapped around me as I sobbed. *What the fuck?* I rarely cried, and I wasn't really sure why I was crying now. I allowed myself to fall apart in my mother's arms for a few minutes before pushing her away and wiping my face with my sleeve.

"Sorry," I hiccupped. "I don't know what came over me."

"I think you've gotten used to hiding your feelings, kiddo, and now they're all bubbling up to the surface. Have you ever thought about talking to someone?" she asked with a wince.

"I don't need a shrink, Mom."

"What's wrong with talking to someone to help you sort out your emotions? Weren't you the one to suggest it to Daphne?"

"This isn't the same. Marcus was manipulating her, and she needed help to see that."

"So you're going to just keep pushing people away?"

"I'm fine, Mom. I don't need therapy. My life is perfectly fine the way it is. I'm happy."

"Whatever you say, bug." She stood and started clearing our plates. "I'm here for you if you ever want to talk or have more questions about your dad, okay?"

"Yeah, okay. I think I'm good for now. I need to process this new information."

THE NEXT NIGHT, I had Daphne over for a much-needed girls' night. It felt like ages since we'd had a night all to ourselves. I was ready with all of her favorite snacks and a bottle of our favorite wine when she arrived.

"So, how was Christmas with your parents?" I asked as we settled into our spots on my couch. "Are they madly in love with Nathan now, too?"

"Har, har. It was nice. And it wasn't too awkward," she chuckled. "You've met Nathan—he's so damn charming. How could they not like him?"

"Yeah, I guess. Did they say anything about how soon it all happened? I remember you saying they thought it was too soon for you to be getting into something after the one who will not be named," I snickered. Daphne didn't share my sense of humor when it came to dickhead, I guess, because she ignored me, *moving on.*

"I think they're warming up to him. It was really nice, actually." Daphne stared off into space, reminiscing.

"My Christmas was great. Thanks for asking," I laughed.

"Shit, sorry. I zoned out there for a minute. Work wasn't a shitshow then?"

"No, thankfully, it was pretty chill, and a few family members brought us food and treats, so that was an added bonus on top of the double time."

"That's good. So what's been going on with you? I feel like we haven't really had a chance to catch up in a while." Daphne pulled her legs up under her and turned toward me, giving me her full attention.

Great. This was my chance to come clean—to tell her about Brandon. My heart raced, and I felt all tingly.

"What's the matter?" she asked, looking serious.

"Nothing… I… It's just that I… Nothing." I stuttered over my words. I needed to tell her the truth, but why was this so hard? I took a big sip of wine.

"Does this have anything to do with you and Brandon?"

My eyes grew wide, and I choked and sputtered on my wine. After a minute of knocking on death's door, I regained the ability to talk. "Why would you say that?"

"You guys have been spending all that time together for your tattoo, and you looked awfully chummy the other night." She didn't look upset, but I kept quiet, hoping she'd do the hard part for me. "But don't go getting any ideas," she joked.

"What's that supposed to mean?" I asked, feeling a little defensive.

"Seriously, Lexi, it would be a total clusterfuck if you guys hooked up. Think about it. Nathan and I are solid, and we'll be spending more holidays and stuff together now. You are my best friend, and Brandon is not only his brother but also one of his closest friends. If you guys actually ended up dating, that would be really cool, but I don't want things getting weird if you hook up and Brandon goes and gets attached." She put her hand on my leg. "I love you, girl, but you're a self-proclaimed fuckgirl. From what I've learned about him, that's not Brandon's style, and he likes you. I can tell, but I don't want him getting hurt."

She was making good points. Even though I wasn't ready for a relationship, I didn't want Brandon to get hurt.

As much as I wanted to come clean to Daphne, maybe I needed to end things with him or, better yet, get over my bullshit and date him like an adult.

<h1 style="text-align:center">28</h1>

<hr>

BRANDON

After spending a few days thinking things over, I decided I was going to just go with the flow with Lexi. If she wanted casual, that's what I was going to give her. I knew I needed to be cautious. Lexi wasn't a woman who needed a man, and I got the feeling she wasn't interested in any traditional relationship, so I needed to approach our situation a bit differently. I needed to keep things casual and fun, showing her how good things could be with us if she would let me in.

New Year's Eve probably wasn't the best day for this, but it was a day she had off, and Daphne and Nathan had other plans, so I figured she'd be free. Since we hadn't spoken since that tense drive back from my dad's on Christmas Eve, I wasn't sure how she would react to my invitation.

ME

Hey, got any plans for New Year's?

LEXI

No. Why, what's up?

ME

I was thinking we could go to the
Basement and have some fun.

LEXI

As long as the night ends in orgasms, I
could be persuaded to have drinks with
you beforehand.

ME

I can definitely promise you will start off
the new year coming all over my dick.

LEXI.

Bet.

That was easier than I expected, but of course, she led with sex stuff. I wondered whether my response was a mistake. But at that point, I needed to put in some time with her outside of the bedroom if this was going to go anywhere, and unfortunately, the only way to do that was to make other promises too.

ON NEW YEAR'S EVE, I offered to pick Lexi up, but she chose to meet me at the bar instead. I believe her exact words were, *'That's too datey.'* Not exactly how I wanted the night to start, but I brushed it off and went to the bar on my own. After securing us a couple of spots at the bar, I ordered us both drinks and waited for her arrival.

The door to the bar opened, and a rush of cool air swept by me. I turned to see Lexi sweep into the place like she owned it. She looked amazing. Her hair, which was usually wavy or poker straight, was now curled and bouncy. She wore red lipstick, and her bright blue eyes popped against her bold black liner. Wearing a black leather jacket over a sequin top that left very little to the imagination, she was a total knockout. A smile broke out on her face as our eyes met, and she strutted to me.

When she reached me, she placed her hand under my chin and pushed my jaw up. I didn't even realize my mouth was hanging open, but I wasn't surprised. She was stunning. "You look beautiful," I choked out.

"Thanks," she said as I pulled her seat out for her. "What a gentleman! Oh, and you remembered my drink," she added.

"I did remember, but this was all Diane. I told her I was meeting you," I confessed.

"Well, I appreciate it all the same. Thank you."

"Thanks for meeting me. I wasn't sure if you would. New Year's Eve is kind of a coupley thing," I said with a wince. *What was wrong with me?* My stupid mouth was going to be my downfall; I knew it.

But Lexi laughed it off, saying, "It's just another day, Brando. Don't make it weird." She was really easygoing and easy to talk to, and seemed to forget any confrontation or tension we'd had up until this point. It made me wonder whether she took anything seriously or if she'd ever felt deeply about anyone before.

My thoughts and mouth were once again at war with my better judgment, as I asked, "So you don't date? Like at all?"

She huffed and turned to face me. "I'm pretty sure we've been over this before, but I don't see the point. I mean, sure, some relationships last, but in my experience, they don't, so why get emotionally invested in something that has an expiration date?"

"That's a pretty grim outlook." I frowned. "And a pretty lonely way to live."

"I'm not lonely," she scoffed. "Can we change the subject, though? I agreed to come out for a fun night of laughs and orgasms, not philosophical discussions about relationships."

Despite my disappointment at her avoiding the topic, I laughed and changed the subject. "So, how about those Birds?"

"Oh, hell no. Ball sports are off the table too," she laughed.

God, I loved her laugh. Even though she was avoiding opening up, I admired her ability to move on so quickly from uncomfortable conversations. "What's your beef with ball sports?" I chuckled.

"Don't get me wrong, if there's a game on and I'm at a bar with a bunch of fans, I can get into the spirit, but I don't know players' names or stats or any of that crap. And don't get me started on those fantasy footballers."

"Ha! Dylan does that shit! I never understood the draw myself, though."

"I never would have pegged him as a fantasy football guy. He seems more likely to play ball sports rather than manage a fake team or whatever it is that they do."

"He played football in high school, actually. Dylan was the most athletic of the three of us. I really thought he'd go off and play in college and maybe even go pro one day. But he decided college wasn't for him and started working in the shop right after high school."

"I could totally see him playing football. Typical jock fuckboy, huh?" she laughed.

I chuckled too, because that pretty much summed Dylan up. "Yeah, I guess so. But art was his first love, and all he ever talked about was working at the shop."

"That's so awesome that you guys all work together and that you love what you do." Lexi finished her drink and waved to get Diane's attention. "Want another beer?" she asked me as Diane approached.

"One more." I finished my beer and pushed the glass across the bar.

Time seemed to fly by when I was with Lexi. Despite my having to stay away from the topics I wanted to talk about most, there was rarely a lull in our conversations. Everything felt easy with her. Well, almost everything. Except for the whole *'she won't date me thing,'* everything else was great.

Before I knew it, the bar was shouting out the count-down to midnight. Lexi was staring at the TV screen above the bar, counting down along with the rest of the bar, a huge smile plastered on her face. She glanced over at me with a few seconds to go. *Was she going to let me kiss her at midnight?*

3... 2... 1... Fuck it.

I pulled Lexi into my arms. She looked up at me, still smiling. "Happy New Year, Brando."

I leaned in close so that our lips were almost touching. "Happy New Year, Sweetheart."

Surprisingly, Lexi was the one who closed the distance between us and kissed me. Maybe it was wishful thinking on my part, but that kiss felt different. It felt as if Lexi was leaving the door open for more.

29

———————

LEXI

It had been weeks since New Year's, and things were going surprisingly well still. I hadn't ended things with him, nor did I start dating him like an adult. *Avoidance Lexi* was still running the show. Thankfully, Brandon and I were keeping things pretty casual, and he still wasn't pressuring me for more. We even made it through Valentine's Day without him pulling any romantic crap. Sometimes we'd meet at one of our apartments, or we'd grab a drink at a local bar beforehand. Nothing too datey, and we still hadn't had any sleepovers. Sometimes I'd catch him looking at me funny. Like he was admiring a piece of art, but mostly he was holding up his end of our arrangement and keeping feelings out of it. If he was catching feelings, he was doing a pretty good job of hiding it, which was fine with me. *Or was it?*

Over the past month, we'd only gotten closer. Although we didn't really dig deep into our pasts, he was quickly becoming someone I'd call a friend. That was definitely a new concept for me—*friends with benefits? I guess it was a step up from fuck buddies?*

What the fuck was wrong with me? Brandon was a great guy. He was funny and kind and could fuck like no one I'd ever been with, and I was pushing him away at every turn. I needed to just chill and be the cool girl. *Go with the flow.*

My thoughts continued to spiral as we walked up the stairs to his apartment. We'd come from having drinks at the Basement, something we did pretty often these days. It was beginning to feel less weird spending so much time with him, and we were having so much fun.

Brandon opened the door and guided me in with his hand on the small of my back. As soon as the door shut, I turned and pushed him up against it, reverting to the only way I knew how to act with a guy. Thankfully, he didn't stop me and leaned down to capture my mouth with his.

"Mmmm, need something, Sweetheart?" Brandon taunted as he lifted me into his arms.

"Yes, you, now," I demanded.

Brandon chuckled against my lips as he carried me to his bedroom. "So needy tonight."

"Tonight?" We both laughed, and then a yelp escaped me as I landed on his bed with a bounce.

"Well, you were a good girl at the bar tonight. Maybe you should get a reward?"

I nodded my head vigorously. I had been on my very best behavior and didn't once try to make him jealous or act bratty. Actually, the thought hadn't even crossed my mind. I was too busy enjoying his company. *Fucking crazy.*

"Strip," he demanded, drawing me out of my thoughts. I slowly undressed while he stood at the foot of the bed with hungry eyes, looking too good to be real. But he was real, and he was all mine. Well, he'd be all mine if I weren't such a fucking mess. *Did I want that?* The more time we spent together, the more the line I'd drawn between us blurred.

When I was fully undressed, Brandon asked, "How do you want it, Sweetheart? It's dealer's choice tonight."

I put my index finger between my teeth, thinking about how I wanted him. At that point, I thought we'd fucked each other in every way possible. Brandon adjusted himself through his jeans. "Better decide soon, or else you'll be in for a punishment."

"Ha! Like that's a bad thing!" I laughed. He moved towards the bed, but I held up my hand. "Wait! I want you to do that thing you did the first night."

"You'll have to be more specific," he chuckled.

"Fingerbang me into oblivion, Brando."

"With pleasure," he answered. He quickly stripped out of his clothes and joined me on the bed.

I lay back and spread my legs to give him access. Maintaining eye contact, he leaned down to inhale my scent. "I've been craving this sweet pussy all damn night, Lexi."

"Mmmm. I've been thinking about this all day, too. Please don't make me wait another minute." My pussy ached for him. His proximity was almost unbearable, and I needed him to touch me.

Too gently, he swiped his tongue through my wetness, and I swear he actually growled. *Damn, that was sexy as hell.*

"More, please, Brandon," I begged, because I knew how much he liked it when I did.

He rewarded me with more pressure and speed. He pushed two fingers into my dripping pussy, almost sending me over the edge. He knew every button to push to get me off, but he also knew when I was getting close and, annoyingly, would usually back off before I'd orgasm. *Hopefully, he'd let me come quickly this time.* My pussy clenched around his thick fingers. I was so close.

With his fingers working my insides roughly, he took my clit into his mouth, sucking it gently and then biting down on it with just the right amount of pressure to send me careening over the edge. I shouted as a fierce orgasm enveloped me. My whole body convulsed, and I reached down to hold Brandon's head in place, desperate to ride this one out.

After my soul returned to my body, I released Brandon's head. He sat back on his heels with a devilish grin. "You liked that?" He leaned over and retrieved a condom from the bedside table.

"You know I did. Don't go getting cocky," I tutted.

"Speaking of cocky," he said as he stroked his cock, rolling the condom over himself.

A giggle escaped me. "You're ridiculous. Now get that anaconda over here and defile me."

That did it. He laughed out loud before tackling me.

Without warning, he was gliding inside me. I didn't think I'd ever get used to his size, but luckily, my pussy was a slip 'n slide and he slid right in.

With one hand on my hip and the other propping him up on the bed, he pounded into me. "Is this what you wanted, Sweetheart?"

"Yes! Fuck yes, Brandon." I shouted as another orgasm crept up on me. His hand on my hip moved to roughly pinch my nipple, sending me over the edge.

"Fuck, when you come, your pussy squeezes me so hard, Lexi. You feel so good." He fucked me through that orgasm and then another, before flipping me onto my stomach and entering me again from behind.

He pulled my hips up and fucked me within an inch of my life. The feel of him stretching me with every thrust had me on the edge again, and as I tipped over into another orgasm, Brandon followed me with his own. He stayed firmly seated inside of me for a few moments until we'd both come down. He leaned over me and whispered into my neck, "I'll be right back." Then jumped out of bed and trotted into the ensuite.

I could keep my head in the game while we were fucking, but afterwards, my mind raced again. *Who did I think I was? There was no way things would last with Brandon. He wouldn't let this be just sex forever, and I didn't know if I could let it be more.* I felt the overwhelming urge to run out of there, but was determined to stay—to actually try with him.

He walked back into the bedroom, grinning. "Oh, you're

still here?" I knew he was joking, but it didn't land as intended, because after just talking myself into giving this a go, I now felt like I'd made a huge mistake.

I moved to get up. "I can leave," I huffed.

He was on me immediately—his body covering mine, making it impossible for me to move. "No. Please, Lexi, stay. It was a bad joke. Shit. I'm sorry."

"Joke or not, that's what I do, right?" I avoided his eyes. "I run away. I mean, why would I want to stick around? You'll tire of this soon enough. Tire of me."

"Hey, look at me." He placed one hand on my cheek, turning my head so I met his gaze. "I know this is hard for you to hear, but you are worth so much more than you give yourself credit for. You deserve to feel special and cared for, and I'm not going anywhere."

"See, that's exactly what makes me want to run. You're too perfect, you make me feel seen like no one ever has, and that scares the shit out of me. If I let you in, I don't think I'd survive losing you. I'm fucked up, Brandon. Something is seriously wrong with me. Why else would I push everyone away?"

"There is nothing wrong with you, Lexi. I think you've been let down in the past, and it's making you hesitant to let someone else in."

"My dad left us when I was a kid," I said barely above a whisper. "If my dad didn't give a shit, why would anyone else?" I couldn't believe I was opening up to him.

"I care about you, but I'm not going to pressure you into anything, okay? Let's just take things as they come, keep things casual. If you want more, we'll go at your pace, and if not, I will respect that."

"Okay, I'll try."

"I'll take it," he said and then kissed my nose and rolled off of me. "Now, get over here and snuggle me."

This fucking guy. "Snuggle you?"

"Yeah, casually, of course," he chuckled.

"You're an idiot." I couldn't help the smile that had crept onto my face. And then I did something that surprised me. I tucked myself in next to Brandon and rested my head on his shoulder.

"It isn't so bad, is it?" he asked as he stroked my back gently.

"It's weird. Honestly, I don't know how to act right now."

"Be yourself. Nothing's changed. We're just two naked people hanging out in bed."

"That makes it sound even weirder, you lunatic." I slapped at his chest. "Why is this spot blank? You have tattoos literally everywhere but here." I pointed to the only tattoo-free spot on him, the spot right over his heart. I'd noticed it before, but never mentioned it.

"You're gonna think it's dumb."

"Probably, but tell me anyway," I urged.

"I wanted to leave a place for when I meet my forever partner. I want to get a tattoo here, over my heart, that represents the one who captures it."

"God, you're so corny, but you're right. I think that's dumb. What happens when the love of your life asks for a divorce?"

"Still so cynical." He kissed the top of my head. "Get some sleep, Sweetheart."

"Here?" Snuggling was one thing; sleeping over was another fucking story.

"I'll make it worth your while in the morning. Now go to sleep." Brandon sounded half asleep already. I could've probably waited for him to fall asleep and bounce, but I willingly stayed wrapped in his embrace and drifted off.

IN THE MORNING, he did in fact make it worth my while. I woke up with his face between my legs. After several orgasms, he tried to convince me to shower with him, but I declined. I'd already made that mistake once. *Baby steps, right?* Showering together was another thing that felt too intimate. I needed to work my way up to those things.

After I shot down the idea of showering together, he let me go first, giving me some privacy. The shower was glorious, except for my damn brain that wouldn't turn the hell off. I couldn't believe I had spent the night with him. I tried to shake off the uneasy feeling building inside me, to no avail. By the time I made my way back into his bedroom, I was stressed to the max.

"Your turn," I said, not meeting his eyes.

"I put a shirt on the bed for you," he said casually. "I'll

be quick. Don't go running off," he laughed. "I'm going to feed you before you go."

"Fiiiiine. I guess I'll let you feed me." I said dramatically, trying to seem unbothered. Meanwhile, inside, I was freaking the fuck out.

I pulled on his shirt that he had left on the bed for me. Although it was freshly laundered and smelled amazing, it offered me little comfort. I paced his room, which now felt too small. Moving into the living room, I spotted his sketchbook on the dining table. Looking for anything to distract me, I sat at the table and opened the book, expecting to see sketches of tattoo ideas and client pieces.

What I saw knocked the breath from my lungs. I flipped through page after page, my chest growing unbearably tighter.

I had to get the fuck out of there. Brandon was clearly more into me than he was letting on. Daphne was right. I was going to break this gentle giant's heart if I kept up my bullshit. He didn't deserve this. He didn't deserve this broken version of me that couldn't give him what he wanted.

I practically ran back into his room, threw on my pants and shoes, grabbed the rest of my things, and ran like I normally do. But not because I wanted to leave before he could leave me, but because I was damaged goods and not enough for this beautiful human.

9 Months Later

30

———

BRANDON

I knew it was her before I even looked up. I'd know her laugh anywhere. Lexi breezed past the cafeteria, laughing with another nurse, unaware of the daggers that pierced my chest with every sound.

It had been nine months since I'd seen her. *I tried. Believe me, I tried.* When she disappeared that morning in March, I texted, I called, and I even went to her apartment —trying to make her see reason. She'd stumbled upon my sketchbook—not the one that housed my general art or my client sketches, but the one I started the day I met her last Halloween. The one filled with drawings of her, of her eyes, of her body. The one that probably made me look like an obsessed lunatic.

When I'd come out of the shower that day, I'd been hopeful. Lexi's spending the night was a tremendous step for her, and I was cautiously optimistic it was the beginning, not realizing then that it was actually the end. When I found my sketchbook open on the dining table, and Lexi and all of her things gone, I knew it had been too much for her. She wanted casual, and when she found my lovesick musings, she bolted. I immediately sprang into action, running out into the snow to catch her, but I was too late.

She ignored my texts, didn't answer my calls, and when I showed up at her place, she told me to leave and forget about her without even opening the door. But how could I, when she consumed my every thought?

I even tried to convince her to come into the shop so I could finish her tattoo, but she wouldn't hear it and blocked my number. I eventually gave up or started respecting her wishes, depending on how you want to see it. Diane said she hadn't even been back to the Basement that she was aware of since the last time she and I had been in together.

One Sunday at my dad's, Daphne mentioned Lexi had taken a leave of absence to take a travel assignment out west. *Was I so horrible that she'd rather go work across the country than risk running into me here in the city?* Old wounds swiftly reopened, and I retreated from the world. The coping mechanisms I'd learned after my mom died and Miranda left were temporarily forgotten.

Thankfully, Dylan recognized the signs of my retreat right away and helped me get back on track. I upped my therapy appointments, threw myself into my work, and even tried dating over the summer—*which was a complete disaster, by the way.* I was going through the motions of living my life, but my thoughts remained focused on Lexi. If she didn't want me, I could deal with that, but I needed closure.

Her up and leaving without a word was the worst thing she could've done, and she probably had no idea of how badly she'd hurt me.

And now there she was, laughing like nothing had happened, while I spent the last nine months in agony. I'd only known this woman for a few months before she disappeared from my life, yet the hole she left in my chest, which had only just started to heal, was now being ripped back open again. I knew volunteering at the hospital this year was a mistake, but I did it anyway—clearly a glutton for punishment.

"Look, Mom, it's Santa!" I heard a young boy exclaim, drawing my attention back to the present.

"Ho, ho, ho!"

KNOWING Lexi had worked that day gave me a pretty good idea of when she'd be getting home that night, so I parked my ass in front of her place like a stalker. I needed answers and closure. If she was done with me, I needed her to say it to my face, and for some sick reason, I needed an explanation.

It was early December, and we hadn't had our first snowfall yet, but that didn't stop it from being colder than hell. I cranked the heat in my car, turned on some tunes, and settled in to wait. Fifteen minutes later, Lexi jumped out of a car in front of her building. I was relieved to see that she hadn't walked home as she often did. It was too cold for her to walk.

I quickly shut off my car and jogged across the street towards her. She must have heard me approaching, because she turned her head just before I reached her. I was not prepared for the smile that overtook her face. I didn't know what I expected, but that wasn't one of the scenarios I'd played out repeatedly in my mind.

"Hey, Brando!" she beamed, but her expression changed quickly, mirroring my own. "What's wrong?"

"What's wrong?" I closed my eyes, attempting to calm myself. *How could she ask me that?* It was as if she didn't know what she'd done to me. As if it hadn't been nine fucking months since I'd seen her. I schooled my features and continued. "Can we talk?"

"Yeah, of course. Come on in," she offered, opening the door. I held it open for her and ushered her inside out of the cold. The walk to her apartment was quiet. The things I had to say didn't include small talk.

After we were inside her apartment, she took off her heavy coat and walked to the kitchen. "Can I get you something to drink, Brandon?"

"I'm good." My jaw ticked. I was ready to get this over with. I didn't want to spend one minute more than necessary in this apartment—in her presence.

"Well, take your jacket off and make yourself comfortable. It's been a day, and I could use a glass of wine. I'm really glad you came by, actually."

"You are? And here I thought you've been avoiding

me," I said flatly, taking a seat on the single chair next to the couch. I didn't think I could bear to sit directly next to her.

She settled into the spot closest to me on the couch. "Yeah, about that. I'm really sorry."

"About what part exactly?"

"All of it, Brandon." She rushed her words out as if I'd leave before she could get it all out. "I was a fucking mess when we met, and that wasn't your fault. You did nothing wrong. In fact, you're the reason I had to leave. I don't mean that it's your fault. I mean, I needed to sort my shit out because I didn't want to hurt you. I know I probably did anyway, and I'm sorry for that, but I was so fucking scared and I didn't want to take you down with me." She sucked in a deep breath and then continued at a slower pace. "Here's the deal. I've never had any romantic relationships before— never even had feelings for someone like that. I avoided relationships because of shit that happened when I was a kid. My dad's leaving *really* fucked me up, but I've only recently come to realize that. So, when we met, and I started to feel something for you, it freaked me the fuck out. And then when I saw those sketches and realized I couldn't give you what you probably wanted, I ran. That was a mistake. Staying and talking to you about it would have been the right thing to do, the mature thing, but I didn't. I wasn't ready."

A tear trailed down her cheek, and I fought the urge to wipe it away. "And you're ready now?" I asked, unsure if I was ready myself.

"I think so."

My patience was wearing thin, and her uncertainty wasn't helping. "Ready for what exactly? For a relationship or to talk things out like an adult?"

"Both?" The question in her answer had me on my feet.

"Cut the shit, Lexi." She watched with wide eyes as I paced around her living room. "If I hadn't come here today and cornered you, you wouldn't even be talking to me right now. Am I right?" I clenched my fists at my sides as I continued to pace.

A sob escaped her, and my need to comfort her almost broke my resolve to get answers. "I wanted to come to you as soon as I got home, but I was so nervous, Brandon. And I wanted to be ready to start something if you were open to it. I'm scared I'm going to fuck this up—I'm afraid I already have." She wiped the tears that littered her cheeks. "I didn't know what to do with all the things I was feeling, so I started therapy when I got back. I wanted to be in a better place before I saw you again."

Hearing that she, too, had been in therapy, stopped me in my tracks. Turning to look at her, I realized this was not the same Lexi who had left me all those months ago. This was a Lexi who was trying to heal from her past—something I was all too familiar with. She was making an effort to better herself, and I was so proud of her, even though I was still hurt and angry about how she'd gone about it.

"And *are* you? In a better place?" I moved to sit next to her on the couch.

"I think so." She peered up at me through wet lashes, nodding.

I placed a hand on her arm, forcing myself to stop there. "Well, I'm happy for you, Lexi. I'm glad you're healing. I wish you'd have talked to me before you left without a word. You don't know what that did to me."

"I know I hurt you."

"You have no idea." Turning away from her, I ran a hand through the hair that had come loose from my elastic. "You're not the only one with abandonment issues, Sweetheart." My pet name for her slipped out effortlessly.

Her hand landed on my back gently, caressing the hurt away. "Oh, fuck Brandon. I didn't think—" She paused, realizing maybe I had my own trauma too. Her demeanor turned somber. "I really am so sorry. There's no excuse for how I acted, and I really hope that you can forgive me. And if you're open to it, I'd like for us to start over."

"I'm not gonna lie, Lex, I was so mad—still am, and I just came here to get some closure because, honestly, I thought we were done."

"And now? Are you done with me?" she asked, sounding hopeful.

"I don't know, Lexi. I don't know if I can trust you. How do you know you're even ready to try again?"

"We won't fuck."

31

LEXI

amn it. All the work I did this summer to stop being such a fuckgirl went right out the window as soon as I saw him. My pussy throbbed at the sight of him on my stoop and the sound of his deep voice. I was determined not to let my pussy run the show this time around, though—Brandon and I needed to talk. *Like for real.* He needed to know why I ran out and how sorry I was, but all I could think of was him punishing me for leaving. *Yes, please!*

No! Down, girl.

Seeing those sketches freaked me the fuck out. That, combined with staying the night and my growing feelings for him, sent me running for the hills. I wasn't used to feeling the way I did, and seeing how much I meant to Brandon scared the crap out of me. Daphne was right. Brandon didn't deserve my half assed attempt to be barely more than fuck buddies. He deserved someone who wasn't broken—someone who was all in. Or at least someone who could give him more than I could.

So I ran. I ran right into the bed of another man. *I know. I know. You're probably thinking, but Lexi, how could you? What about Brando?* But let's face it. Some people eat their feelings—I fuck mine right out of my system. So, in true Lexi fashion, I went out and did what I always do. I found some random guy to help numb the pain. I actually even felt a little bad for that guy. Before either of us finished, I ended up bursting into tears and getting the fuck out of there. That was my rock bottom. That was when I knew I needed to make a change. I needed to deal with my shit and I needed time and space to do that.

My first call was to Daphne. I didn't tell her specifically about Brandon, but led with the fact that I needed a break from life and, in so many words, needed to deal with my unresolved daddy issues. Being the supportive bestie that she is, she listened to my blubbering. She offered perfectly reasonable suggestions—none of which included bailing on my life and taking a travel assignment three thousand miles away.

Was running away the most mature thing I could have done? Nope. But that's what I did. I took a three-month leave of absence from work and picked up a travel assignment somewhere the temperature wasn't below freezing. There was sun, sand, and not one reminder of Brandon's beautiful face. It should have been delightful, but it was so depressing. I missed Daphne and the other gals from work. I missed my mom, and I missed Brandon. The three months I was away were spent working and living in a perpetual state of general avoidance.

After my assignment ended, I came home, and that's when the actual work began. I went to therapy and worked my shit out like a real-life adult. *Fucking wild. Who was I even?* All those nights fucking random dudes, telling myself I was okay being alone, turned out to be a lie I told myself over and over again. In reality, I was lonely and afraid of rejection. It's amazing what endless hours of therapy can teach you.

Anyway, I finally felt ready to get on with my life. There was just one problem, and his name was *Brandon Pierce*. Every time over the last few months that I thought about reaching out, I chickened out. I felt so nervous to put myself out there, but I also felt ashamed of how I'd left things with him, and I feared he wouldn't be able to forgive me, or even worse, that he'd moved on with someone else.

Now he was sitting in my living room, looking too damn good, and I couldn't fucking believe the words that were coming out of my mouth.

"We won't fuck," I blurted out, surprising myself.

"And that means I can trust you not to run away again?" he laughed.

"Think about it. My go-to M.O. has been to fuck and run, for lack of a better term. If there's no fucking—and we actually date each other like adults—then there's no reason to run, right?"

"I'm not seeing the logic here. You could still run. I think the feelings part is what spooked you."

"I've been doing a lot of work over the last few months. Therapy has been really good for me, and I'm ready. I didn't reach out because, honestly, I was afraid you hated me."

"I could never hate you, Lexi, but you have to talk to me. Tell me what you're thinking. You can't up and leave again."

"I won't. I promise." And I actually meant it. I wanted to try not only for him but for myself. I deserved to have someone in my life, and if that person wasn't Brandon, then this would be good practice for the next time. Although I really hoped Brandon was the first and last guy I'd have to actually date. *Gah, my therapist would be so proud of me.*

"How about this? We start over. Take our time. And like you said, no sex. Let's get to know each other without the pressure or expectations of sex or labels."

"I can do that." I let out a breath. After all these months of anxiety building up to this moment, I was relieved that I was finally having this conversation with him. "And you're right; the thought of jumping back in where we left off feels a little stressful. Two people just getting to know each other is a little less anxiety-provoking." I let out a small laugh, the stress I'd been holding on to for months beginning to fade.

"And we agree to complete honesty, no matter what. Whatever you're feeling, I want to know, and vice versa." He leveled me with a look that said he meant business.

I reached my hand out between us. "Deal."

He took my hand in his and gave it a soft squeeze. "Deal."

I reclined back onto the couch after he released my hand and took a big sip from my wine glass. "So, whatcha been up to?"

His laughter echoed through my apartment. "God, I missed you and your uncanny ability to change gears."

Hand to my chest, I shot back, "I'm sure I don't know what you mean, sir."

He raised an eyebrow. "Better cut 'sir' out of your vocabulary while we are working on being friends, Lexi."

"Or what?" I batted my eyelashes. *Didn't we just agree no sex?* Yet, there I was, going back to my default settings.

He ignored my bratty comment and avoided my eyes. "Well, since we're being honest, I upped my therapy appointments and I've been working a lot."

"I didn't know you went to therapy. Because of your mom? Shit. You don't have to talk about it if you don't want to." I didn't want to pry, but if we were friends or trying to be, that's something I'd ask a friend.

"Yeah, partially. When my mom was sick, I was in a relationship with a woman I honestly thought I'd end up marrying. But she showed her true colors and up and left when I needed her the most. Losing my mom and her at the same time was a lot, and I didn't handle it well at all." He paused as if he wanted to say more and was deciding whether to continue. "It was bad, Lexi."

"Fuck. I'm sorry, Brandon. I had no idea." The realization of what I'd done hit me like a ton of bricks. I wasn't used to dealing with the aftermath of my actions when it came to men. I usually got what I needed and moved on with my life. With the consequences of my actions staring me in the face, I felt a heaviness in my chest that I hadn't felt before.

"How could you have? It's not like our conversations ever got that deep or personal. We both had our secrets—our own issues. Now that they're out on the table, we can move forward."

I winced, remembering I still had one more secret to share, fearing it would be too much for Brandon to deal with. We agreed to be honest with each other, so I pulled on my proverbial big-girl panties. "Speaking of secrets—" I started, looking down at my wineglass. "In the spirit of laying all our cards on the table, I have something I should tell you."

He looked over at me expectantly, waiting for me to divulge my secret.

I sat up straighter and gathered my courage. With my heart beating out of my chest, I went on, "I slept with someone else."

Taking a deep breath, his nostrils flared, and his eyes closed, but he remained silent, so I continued.

"It was a couple of days after I ran out on you. Not my finest moment, but I fell back on the only coping mechanism I knew to numb the pain I was feeling. It was a mistake—one that I regret so much—and I thought you should know. But I haven't been with anyone since."

Brandon was so still, I wasn't sure if he'd even heard me. I didn't plan on telling him about my rock bottom, but it felt dishonest to keep it from him. And since we agreed on honesty and friendship, I needed to come clean.

With his eyes still closed and fists clenched at his sides, he breathed, "It's fine."

"It was my rock bottom, Brandon. I felt horrible, which was new for me. I'd never regretted my whorish ways until that moment. I—"

"Stop." He interrupted my poor excuse for an apology tour. His pacing resumed as he continued, "I don't want to hear another word about it. You left; we weren't together, but the thought of you with someone else makes my blood boil, Lexi. I wish I hadn't just agreed to the whole no-sex thing, because all I want to do is fuck you so hard so that you never forget who that pussy belongs to again."

Oh, shit. Pulse. Pulse. Pulse. My whore of a pussy throbbed her approval. Apparently, this possessive side of Brandon did it for me. Why did I suggest no sex again? I licked my lips, my mouth suddenly feeling like the Sahara. "Brandon—"

"I've gotta get out of here." His jacket was already halfway on.

I was on my feet and pulling at his arm before I could stop myself. "Wait. Don't go, please."

He turned to me and grabbed both my arms. "I have to. I can't be here right now, Sweetheart." He leaned down and rested his forehead on mine. "Because if I stay, I *will* fuck you, and I don't want either of us to fuck this up again." The anguish in his voice told me he meant what he was saying. I needed to let him leave, even though, for maybe the first time in my life, I wanted a man to stay and not even for the promise of sex.

"Go," I whispered.

32

BRANDON

Ripping myself away from her took every scrap of my willpower. I went there for answers—to get closure—but instead I was running out of there with more hope than was healthy for someone like me. Someone desperate to find and hold on to love. Years of therapy had taught me a lot of coping mechanisms and how to set realistic expectations when it came to others, but all the therapy in the world couldn't make me walk away from Lexi. She had a hold on me I couldn't shake, not that I wanted to.

After I left her apartment that night, I went home and swiftly dealt with the raging hard-on I'd left there with and went to bed. I awoke the next morning to a text from Lexi.

> LEXI
>
> Hey, just making sure we're good? You
> ran out of here like your ass was on fire
> last night.

ME

Yeah, we're good. I'm glad we're starting over. I guess you unblocked me.

LEXI

Yeah, sorry about that too. I was a mess and couldn't bear hearing from you, but I also didn't want to know when you gave up. That would've hurt as bad.

ME

You working today?

LEXI

No, I'm off today. You?

ME

I'm volunteering at the hospital, and then I've got a few clients this afternoon. Can I take you out tonight?

LEXI

Like on a date?

ME

Yes, Lexi, like on a date.

LEXI

Fine, but I'm still me. Just because I agreed to try with you doesn't mean I can tolerate too much mushy crap.

I laughed out loud. She hadn't changed as much as I thought, but that was a good thing. I didn't want a different version of her; I just wanted her to let me in. I wanted us to grow together. If that meant I had to dial back the romance, so be it.

ME

Noted. Dial back the romance.

LEXI

I'm probably going to regret this, but you do you. If it's too much, I'll let you know.

ME

Really?

ME

Nevermind. Forget that. I'll pick you up at 8.

LEXI

Okay, see you then.

I put the phone back down on the bedside table and grinned into my pillow. I couldn't believe how the last twenty-four hours had gone. We were really going to give this a go, and I was excited to see how it would play out. Without sex clouding either of our judgments, I was confident we could make it work.

I ARRIVED at Lexi's place just before eight o'clock with a bouquet of flowers in hand. Initially, I thought about skipping the flowers, but Lexi had told me to do my thing. So there I was standing at her door with flowers, overflowing with nervous excitement. I knocked on the door and held my breath. It still felt as if this wasn't actually going to happen. I'd run through so many scenarios of how this would go—many of which ended with Lexi slamming the door in my face.

She opened the door moments later, and all of my uneasiness floated away.

"Wow," I said, taking her in from head to toe. She wore a curve-hugging sweater dress and knee-high boots and had her hair and makeup done to perfection.

As I was searching for an appropriate compliment to describe how good she looked, Lexi smoothed her hands over her dress. "Is it too much? Should I change?"

"Change? Never. You look incredible."

"I never wear dresses, but I also never date… sooooo." She did a little flourish with her hands, gesturing to her outfit. "Ta-da!"

"It's perfect. Really, you look great. Here, these are for you," I said as I pushed the flowers into her hands.

The look of horror on her face made me second-guess the gesture for the hundredth time today. "Too much?" I parroted her sentiments about her attire.

She schooled her features before raising her eyes to mine. "No, sorry. They're beautiful. This is nice. It's just—" She paused to chew her lip. Her very plump, very kissable lip. *Fucking stop it. Behave.* "I don't think anyone's ever given me flowers before except for my mom when I graduated nursing school."

"Are you okay?" I couldn't make out what was going on in that beautiful head of hers.

"This is weird." *Oh, fuck me.* The flowers were too much. I knew I should have dialed it back.

"Shit, I'm sorry. If it's too much, I can—" I reached for them, but Lexi hugged them to her chest.

"Don't you dare. Just because this is weird as shit, doesn't mean I don't want them." She turned and walked into the kitchen. I followed her, closing the door behind me.

A laugh escaped me, and I shook my head as I reached where she was rummaging through a cabinet. "What's weird exactly?"

"All of it. We're going on a freaking date, Brando. My first date. Like ever."

"What? You didn't go on any dates when you were in school?"

"Nope. Not a one." Lexi pulled a pint glass out of a cabinet and eyed it skeptically. "Think this will work?" She put the glass next to the flowers to measure and then put it back and continued her hunt for something to put the flowers in.

"Let's circle back to the fact that you've never been on a date." Stopping her search, she turned to look at me.

"Look, it's not a big deal. Let's not make it a whole thing, okay?" Lexi turned back to her task. "Oh, shit, this should work." Triumphantly, she spun around with a large pitcher in her hand. "I usually use this for margs, but it'll have to do." She filled the pitcher with water and arranged the flowers in it. "So where are we going?"

"It's a surprise."

"Ugh, you're so annoying, but fiiiiiiine. Let's go before

I change my mind. You'd better be feeding me, though, because I'm fucking starving."

"So you're telling me you won't eat *any* yellow candy?" I wiped a tear from the corner of my eye. We'd been laughing practically non-stop since we arrived at the restaurant. Things were definitely going better than I had expected, and my nerves were gone.

"I don't know why anyone *would*. They're disgusting. It's like eating freaking kitchen cleaner."

"But you like lemons?"

"They're not mutually exclusive, Brando. Lemon candy has a fake lemon flavor and tastes like shit. Real lemons are delicious."

"Do you want another margarita before we go to the next location?" I asked her, eyeing her empty glass.

"What next location? I thought this was the date."

"It's only the first stop. Wait, you thought a Mexican restaurant was the surprise?"

"Well, it was a surprise since I didn't know where we were going. But now that you've told me there's more, let's get out of here. I can't wait to see what you've got in store for me."

I paid the bill, and we left the restaurant, heading towards the subway instead of my car.

"If you tell me the surprise is taking the subway, Brandon, I'm going to have to pass. Been there, done that, and I am not a fan. You know, a guy once jerked off onto an oncoming train from the platform right in front of me? It was terrifying and impressive at the same time."

I was laughing so hard my face hurt. "Holy shit. For real?"

"Yeah, the subway is a wild place, not for the faint of heart, but hey, if that's how you want to spend this date, who am I to judge?" She shrugged and swiped her card, moving through the turnstile before I could pay for her.

I quickly caught up with her. "You should've let me pay for the subway."

"Why? Listen, I let you get dinner, but just because we're on a date, doesn't mean you have to pay for everything or that I'm now suddenly helpless."

I shook my head. "Believe me, I'd never call you helpless, but I want to take care of you tonight. Can you let me do that?"

"You're really testing my limits, but I'll try."

AS WE APPROACHED our final destination for the evening, a block away from where we got off the subway, I turned to watch Lexi's reaction.

"Are you fucking kidding me right now?" Lexi was bouncing up and down, clearly excited about our next activity. "I've always wanted to do this!"

After checking in at the front desk and securing ourselves a couple of drinks from the bar, we made our way to our assigned lane. While a staff member went over some instructions and did a brief demonstration, Lexi was practically chomping at the bit to get started. She bounced from one foot to the other, constantly moving.

"My turn?" she asked excitedly, when the staff member had finished their demonstration.

"Here ya go," he said, handing Lexi the axe.

Lexi gripped it and gave me a wink. *Oh, fuck, maybe handing her a weapon was a bad idea.*

Thwack. Dead center. "Ha! You're going down, Brando!"

33

LEXI

"I can't believe he bought you a fucking cabin?"

Daphne's laugh echoed throughout the cabin. "He didn't buy *me* a cabin. It's an investment."

"Bullshit, girlie pop. Nate Dog's got it bad for you." The cabin was amazing—the perfect retreat from the city. We were going to have so much fun here in the summer. I was looking out the back window, imagining myself floating on a raft in the middle of the lake, when Daphne came to stand next to me.

"It's pretty great, huh?"

"It's perfect. I can't wait for summer. You, me, floaties, and margs. Say less!" I wrapped an arm around my bestie. She invited me here for a girls' weekend to help her get the place ready for Christmas, and I was more than willing to help. But we also needed this time to reconnect. My little menty b last winter put too much space between us both physically and emotionally, and I thought it was about time for me to come clean. The Lexi that pushed people away was on her way out, never to be seen again. At least I hoped so.

"Fall will always be my favorite, but you're right, I'm excited for summers here too." Daphne moved into the kitchen. "Want something to drink?"

I joined her in the large open kitchen. "Nah, I'm good for now. So, what's our plan of attack?"

"Let's get all the stuff out of the car first, and then I can figure out where everything will go."

HOURS LATER, we'd put a pretty significant dent in the decorations, but still had half-full boxes of decor strewn about the space.

"Okay, I'm toast. How about we call it for today?" Daphne said as she plopped onto the couch.

"Sounds good to me. I think it's wine-o'clock anyway." I called from the kitchen, where I was already uncorking a bottle of our favorite red.

"Yes, please! We deserve it."

I handed Daphne her glass and joined her on the couch. "The place looks great, Daphne, really. And I'm so happy for you." I raised my glass. "Here's to you and Nate Dog and your beautiful future."

Daphne eyed me suspiciously, but clinked her glass against mine. "California changed you."

"What do you mean?" I wondered if she really saw a difference in me since I'd gone away.

"Babe, I love you, but something's been up with you for a while. You up and left in March and haven't really been yourself since. And now a toast to me, Nathan and our beautiful life? Come on. Spill it. What's going on with you?"

I took a deep breath. Confessing was something I knew I had to do. I'd wanted to for a while, but most times when we were together, Nathan was around or we were at work. *No, that's a lie I'd been telling myself, too.* Truthfully, the fear of losing my best friend had kept me quiet. She told me not to hurt Brandon, and that's exactly what I'd done. But as my therapist loved to tell me, I can't control how others will react to my actions, but I can control my actions. And coming clean was the first step to rebuilding the trust I'd broken with Daphne—even if she didn't know it was broken.

I turned to face her, tucking my legs up underneath me. "Sooooo, remember how you told me not to fuck Brandon?"

"Oh sweet baby Cheesus, Lexi. You didn't!" She palmed her face.

"I did. And then I did exactly what you said I'd do—I hurt him. Things were getting kinda serious, and I freaked out and I ran. I ran all the way to California." Rushing my words, I continued, feeling an overwhelming need to get it all out. "I was a fucking mess. I liked him. Like, I really liked him, and it made me really uneasy. I was afraid I'd gotten too close. I was afraid of falling for him. So I took that leave of absence, thinking that if I put some distance between us, I'd get over it. But I didn't. I thought about him every freaking day. So when I got back, I started seeing a therapist to find out what the fuck was wrong with me. My dad leaving when I was little obviously fucked me up, and seeing my mom sad all the time didn't help. But as it turns out, Mom's been fucking fine this whole time, and get this —dating. Nevermind. That's for another time. The point is, I wanted to figure out why I was such a fuckgirl and why I had such a hard time letting people in." A tear slid down my cheek. "I at least wanted to learn how to open myself up more. I realized I didn't want to be alone forever. And I know you told me not to, and I know I fucked up, but please know that I'm so sorry. I never meant to lie to you or keep things from you. I wanted to tell you so many times, but I was so afraid of losing you. You're the only person I've ever really let in before."

Daphne pulled me into a hug. "Oh, Lexi. Please don't cry. It's okay."

I sobbed into her neck. "Really?"

She pulled away from me to look me in the eye. "You're my best friend, bitch, and I love you. Did you mess up? Yes. But I don't know why you didn't just tell me from the jump."

"Let's see..." I ticked off each point on a finger. "I fucked Nathan's brother after you *specifically* told me not to, then I lied to your face about it, and worst of all, I did exactly what you said I'd do and the whole reason you wanted me to stay away from him in the first place—I hurt Brandon. I was so afraid you'd be pissed, and I didn't want to lose you, too."

"Okay, all of that is bad, and I'm not thrilled about you lying to me, but I don't think I really gave you an opportunity to tell me. If I'm not mistaken, I mentioned a few times what a mess it would be if you two hooked up, but I shouldn't have said anything. It wasn't my place, and I'm sorry."

"No, you were right. I wasn't interested in a relationship then, and I wasn't in the right headspace to be getting involved with him or anyone, for that matter. He's too good, and he didn't deserve what I did or how I treated him." I wiped my eyes.

"God, I was such an asshole, and I feel terrible, Lex. I love you so much." She pulled me into another hug.

"I love you too." I sat back and sipped my wine. "And you weren't an asshole. You were calling me out on my bullshit, and I was being selfish. Thankfully, I'm in a better place now."

"I'm happy for you, babe." She took a sip from her glass before continuing. "I thought it was weird that we didn't see him much this summer. He was probably avoiding anything where you might have been invited, but you were avoiding me like the plague, too. I thought something was off, but I couldn't put my finger on it. Oh, fuck, is it going to be weird at Christmas?"

"I'm not sure. I think I made it right, or at least I'm trying to. We're… um… dating?"

"Is that a question?"

I chuckled. "Yeah. We're trying to take things slow, but we've been out a few times."

"And how do you feel about that?" Daphne asked.

"Things have been really good, I think. We have a lot of fun together, and it's been weird but nice getting to know each other with our clothes on."

Daphne laughed. "Oh, there she is."

"I know. It's so weird, right? I can't believe I'm actually having *clothes on* fun with a man, especially a man I've already fucked six ways from Sunday."

Daphne placed her hands over her ears. "La la la la."

"It's not like you've never heard about my exploits before."

"He's Nathan's brother, Lexi! I do not need the details."

I arched a brow. "So you don't want to know about his magical monster cock?"

Daphne made a gagging sound and then practically shouted, "Fuck no! Don't ever say that again, or I *will* drown you in this lake! Capeesh?"

"Okay, okay. So, you're really not mad?" I winced.

Daphne took my hands in hers. "I'm not mad, but like I said, I'm a little upset you didn't come to me sooner. I would have liked to help you through it. I'm sad that you've been keeping it all in and dealing with this all on your own. Does your mom know at least?"

"Yeah, she's been great. I was glad I had her these past

few months, but I've missed you so much. I'm really so sorry."

"Stop apologizing. But please don't shut me out again. That's what best friends are for—to get us through tough times. I'm here for you, babe, no matter what."

"I won't. I promise. And I mean it this time, I swear. There's one more thing, though."

"Oh, fuck. What now?"

"Can we keep this between us for now?"

"Like I can't tell Nathan? I don't know about that, Lex." The concerned look on her face had me almost regretting asking her, but Brandon and I wanted to keep our relationship to ourselves for now. I told him I was going to tell Daphne, but he wanted to give us a little more time before his whole family started harassing us.

"Just until after the holidays. We are really trying to give it a go, but if I fuck it up again, I don't want his whole family to hate me." That was the truth. I wanted to minimize the number of people who knew so that I wouldn't be a total pariah if shit went south again.

"I'm sure everyone would be so happy for you guys. And you won't fuck it up, but if things don't work out between you two, no one will hate you either."

"You're probably right, but we aren't ready. We aren't even having S. E. X. yet."

Daphne's eyes were wide. "Wow, you must really like him."

I slapped her arm. "Jesus, like I'm such a slut. Okay, okay. I *was*. But I'm really trying to be better."

"Okay. I'm going to keep my yap shut to Nathan about it for now, but I can't keep your secret forever. That's not how I roll with him."

"You're the best, and I promise it won't be too long. Just let us get through the holidays, and then we'll tell everyone."

34

BRANDON

Christmas Eve

The drive to Nathan's cabin was a blur. Dylan and my dad yapped about work most of the way, while I was distracted. This was the first time since last year that I'd see Lexi with our families present. I wondered if I'd be able to keep it together or if we'd be outed. Lexi had already come clean to Daphne, and Dylan knew about us, but they both agreed to let us keep our secret for now. Lexi wanted to get through the holidays without the added pressure of our relationship going public—a relationship that was going surprisingly well.

I'd be lying if I said I hadn't been nervous to start things back up with her, but since agreeing to this whole dating and no sex thing, we've had a lot of fun and gotten much closer. In the few short weeks since we started back up, I saw so many positive changes in Lexi that I was sure we were well on our way to taking things to the next level. I didn't want to rush things, but the sexual tension between us was becoming almost unbearable.

Snow blanketed the driveway of the cabin, the perfect backdrop for our Christmas celebration. Nathan even put up some Christmas lights and decorations. I wouldn't be surprised if that was Daphne's idea, seeing as how Nathan wasn't usually big into Christmas like Mom and I were.

We were kicking the snow off our boots on the porch when Nathan opened the door to greet us. "Hey guys! Glad you could make it. Come on in."

Dad wrapped Nathan in a hug. "Wouldn't miss it for the world, son."

"Yeah, thanks for the invite. I'm excited to see the place." Dylan was next and greeted him with a fist bump.

I hugged Nathan, giving his back a slap. "Feels like we haven't seen much of you lately. I can't wait to see what you've done to the place."

We made our way into the living area, where Daphne was waiting to greet us each with a hug of her own. She had really become an integral part of our family over the last year, and we all loved her. It was so great to see how well she and Nathan were getting on. I'd never seen Nathan happier.

"Can I get you guys something to drink?" Nathan asked as a knock sounded at the door. We each muttered our responses while Daphne went to get the door.

"Hey bitch! Merry fucking Christmas!" Lexi's voice rang out through the space, and I instantly tensed. We'd talked about how this would go down, but as the moment approached, the thought of seeing her here was suddenly overwhelming.

"I think it's wine o'clock!" Lexi called as she breezed past me without even a sideways glance and went to grab a glass.

I bit my lip to keep myself from reacting, but she looked so fucking good, I was having a hard time sticking to our plan. Dressed in leggings and a cropped sweater, I had to tear my eyes away from her plump ass. All I wanted to do was bury my face there.

Gathered by the kitchen island, we spent a few minutes catching up and making small talk. Not long after that Daphne's parents arrived, and we all sat down for dinner. I didn't try to sit next to Lexi, but that's just how things worked out. I kept my eyes and hands to myself mostly, only stealing a look when she was talking so as not to seem like I was being rude. She seemed unfazed by our proximity, though, causing me to second-guess her feelings towards me yet again.

After dinner and dessert, Dad and Daphne's parents took off to a cabin down the road where they were staying, and the rest of us went to get into our comfy clothes, *per Daphne's request*. After changing into sweatpants and a long-sleeved tee, someone pulled me by the arm to the side of the stairs while I was coming down from the loft.

"What the—" I was cut off as Lexi pulled me to her by the collar and kissed me. This was not like the tentative kisses we'd shared over the last few weeks. This kiss was full of passion and longing. *Fucking finally.*

I returned her kiss, delving deeper into her mouth, exploring every inch. She moaned quietly into me, causing my cock to grow hard. I pressed into her, and she lifted a leg and wrapped it around me, drawing me closer still.

"I want you," she whispered. "This whole pretending we don't know each other thing is so fucking hot, Brando."

I chuckled against her cheek. "Careful, Sweetheart. Keeping this a secret was your idea, remember? If you keep this up, we're bound to get caught."

"Fine. But after everyone goes to sleep, you'd better get your ass to my room."

Then, she was gone. Looking around, I was thankful no one was close by. I needed a minute to get my raging hard-on under control. I was wishing I still had jeans on, because these sweatpants weren't doing me any favors in hiding the effect Lexi had on me. When I had everything sorted out, I rejoined the others in the living room, where they were gathered around the coffee table.

"What do you think, brother, Cards Against Humanity or Bullshit?" Nathan asked as I took a seat on the floor across the table from Lexi.

AFTER A FEW HYSTERICAL rounds of *Cards Against Humanity,* it was Dylan's turn to be the card czar, and as he pulled a black card from the pile, he chuckled, "I still can't believe you bought this place."

Lexi chimed in, "I can't wait for a summertime invite. This snow crap isn't really my thing."

"The snow's not so bad when you've got a cozy fire and good company," I added, giving her a wink.

She rolled her eyes. Dismissing me, she turned toward Daphne. "I expect summer beach parties."

Daphne laughed, "Yeah, okay, I think we can make that happen, right, babe?" She beamed at my brother.

"Of course." He leaned down, kissing her.

"Gross, get a room," Dylan huffed.

"Great idea." Nathan scooped Daphne up and carried her to their room. "See ya in the morning!" He called over his shoulder as Lexi, Dylan, and I hooted and hollered after them.

"I guess you two will be sneaking off to do some canoodling of your own then?" Dylan teased as he started cleaning up the cards.

"I don't know *what* you're talking about, Dylan," Lexi said with a roll of her eyes.

"Cut the crap, you two." Dylan set the cards down. "Anyone with eyes can see that the two of you are back at it. Just don't break his heart again, okay, Lexi?"

"Hey, that's not fair. It's not all Lexi's fault things that went the way they did. I was rushing things, and neither of us was ready." I came to Lexi's defense.

She chimed in. "I know I handled things poorly, Dylan, and I'm sorry for that. Brandon knows how sorry I am, too, and we're going slower this time. I'm really trying not to fuck it up again."

"Whatever. I've said what I had to say. You two are adults. Do whatever you want." Dylan got up. "I'm going to bed. See you guys in the morning."

"Goodnight," Lexi and I said almost in unison.

Once Dylan was halfway up the stairs, the energy in the room seemed to shift. Lexi and I stared at each other across the table, unmoving except for our breaths. Mine were ragged, and every breath felt like a chore. I wanted to turn the table over and cross the room to her, but we were in someone else's home and had an agreement between us—an agreement that I was struggling to uphold at that moment.

35

LEXI

"My room, now," I whispered as I moved to get up, but Brandon grabbed my arm across the table, stopping me.

"What about our no-sex clause?" he said through gritted teeth. I knew he wanted to say, *fuck it*, too, but I also understood his hesitation. It had only been a few weeks since we'd started this whole friends-first relationship, and while things were going really well, I was still afraid that sleeping with him again so soon would fuck everything up.

I looked into his eyes and gave him a sly smile. "Who said anything about sex?"

He raised an eyebrow at me. "Oh, my bad. Between that kiss earlier and the tone in which you *demanded* I come to your room, I assumed that's what you meant. Did I misinterpret your intentions, Sweetheart?"

His stupid nickname for me had finally stopped

annoying me, but then it only got me hotter for him—as if that were possible. "Come with me, okay?"

"Okay," he agreed, and we walked to my room. Once safely inside, I locked the door and stood with my back against it. Brandon crowded into my space. Leaning down, he breathed into my ear, "What now?"

I clenched my legs tightly together, attempting to relieve the tension building there. "Why are you making this so hard?"

"I think that's my line," he chuckled.

I burst out laughing. "You're such an idiot."

"An idiot with a raging hard-on thanks to you," he chuckled, and pressed into me, making me very aware of the effect I had on him.

I moved a hand between us to palm his erection, causing him to groan. "Baby, you'd better stop, or I don't think I'll be able to stop myself. And trust me when I say, then everyone in this cabin will know about us."

"Oh, Brando," I said as I rubbed his cock through his sweatpants. "There are lots of things we can do that aren't sex."

Brandon's crumbling resolve gave way, and then his mouth was on mine. Tangled in a ferocious kiss, we pawed at one another. We moved in sync until he was on top of me in the bed.

All I wanted was to give in and fuck this man's brains out, but I was determined to stick to the plan—*at least for now. Sucking his cock surely didn't count, right? Maybe just some moist humping? Was that a thing? It definitely wouldn't be dry humping because I was already soaked.*

"Sweetheart, we are getting dangerously close to crossing the line," Brandon breathed into my mouth as his dick rubbed just where I needed it.

"Keep your clothes on," I rushed out, grinding myself up into him.

"Fuck, Lexi. You feel so good. Fuuuuck." His hand reached under my top and palmed my breast, causing me to arch into him. "Is this okay?" he asked, seeing how far I was willing to go. It was my idea to bring him in here, but what exactly did I want to happen? Old Lexi would have already had him balls deep in her, but I was trying my best not to lead with my whore of a vagina anymore.

"Yeah, that's great. Wait, no, sit up against the headboard."

Brandon reluctantly moved off of me and towards the headboard, pulling his shirt off and tossing it to the floor as he went. "Didn't I just tell you to keep your clothes on?" I chuckled as I began crawling towards him.

"It's hot in here, and besides, my dick is still safely tucked away in these flimsy sweatpants." He snickered and palmed his cock through his pants. "Lexi, maybe I should go upstairs."

I licked my lips. "Brandon, I need to come. It's been far too long."

"But you want us to keep our clothes on?"

"Is that okay?" I asked as I straddled him, his hands gripping my waist.

"Of course, Sweetheart. We're going to go at your pace. I want this to work, and I'm willing to wait as long as you need."

"Honestly, I don't want to wait." I rolled my hips, rubbing myself against his hard length. "I want you to fuck my brains out, but I also know that we made this arrangement because we both didn't want to fall into old habits." Continuing to grind myself into him, I let out a small moan. "I really like you, Brando, and I don't want to fuck up how things have been going, but I need to come. Like I really need it. I'm wound so fucking tight." I ran my hands down his chest, appreciating every ripple of muscle.

"I've got you, Lexi." He lifted his hips, his cock putting the perfect amount of pressure on my sensitive clit.

"Oh, fuck, Brandon. That feels so good."

His hands grabbed my ass roughly, pulling me closer. With our faces close, he demanded, "Use me, Sweetheart. I want you to grind that perfect pussy of yours on my cock until you come." *Oh, fuck yeah!*

Had hotter words ever been said? My pussy clenched at nothing, begging to be filled, but this would have to do for now. I started at a slow, steady pace, rubbing my clit against him. I bit my lip, stifling a moan.

"Let it out, baby. I want to hear how good this feels," he growled and then jerked his hips up into me again, causing my breath to catch.

Determined to come quickly and put myself out of my misery, I placed my hands on his shoulders and picked up my pace. Brandon's breaths were ragged, his cock growing impossibly harder.

"Oh my God, you feel so good," I called out—a little louder than I meant to.

"That's right, Lex. Let go. Come all over me." His hands were everywhere. Teasing my nipples, gripping my thighs, and dragging me roughly against him.

I was ready to pop—*so fucking close*. He gripped my neck and pulled me in for a frenzied kiss, pushing me further into his erection.

He pressed his forehead to mine. "Fuck, Lexi, I'm gonna come." Brandon's words sent me over the edge. My orgasm came crashing through me, sending shockwaves throughout my whole body. My head fell back as I rode out the seemingly endless waves of pleasure.

My body fell against Brandon's as he ground out his own release. "Jesus Christ," he laughed. "I can't believe I just came in my pants."

I chuckled into his chest. "Seriously, how old are we?"

He kissed my temple. "Well, you said we had to keep our clothes on. I just didn't expect a full-on dry hump session."

I sat up to look at him. "There was *nothing* dry about that, I assure you."

Suddenly, I was being lifted off his lap, and he reposi-tioned us so that we were lying on our sides facing one another.

I started to get up, but he stopped me. "Where do you think you're going?"

"I was going to clean up quick. It's a mess down here." I motioned to my crotch.

"We can get cleaned up in a bit. Just lie here with me for a few minutes."

I groaned but lay back down. We stared at each other for a minute before I looked away. He brushed a strand of hair from my face and then turned my chin, forcing my gaze back to his. "I know this is hard for you. Even though we kept our clothes on, you're used to running for the hills after you come. Tell me what's going on in that beautiful head of yours." His thumb caressed my cheek, and then he pulled my leg up over his hip, drawing me in closer.

I looked at the ceiling, trying to gather my thoughts. He was right. I had wanted to run.

"Lexi."

"This *is* hard for me, okay? I have feelings for you that I don't know how to deal with. You're right, though. My first thought was to get the fuck out of here. But truthfully," My gaze settled back onto his beautiful face. "I like you, and spending time with you these past few weeks has actually been a lot of fun."

"Why do I feel like there's a but coming?"

"But old habits die hard. I've done the work and talked about all of this in therapy, but this is definitely a test for me. That I'm still here and having this conversation, I think, says something though."

"It does. I'm proud of you."

I slapped at him. "Oh God, stop it."

He grabbed my hand and placed it over the blank space on his chest. "I'm serious, Lexi. Your staying and talking with me proves that you're really trying, and I'm so proud of you for that."

"Thank you. Now, can we please get cleaned up before I give myself a UTI?"

The next thing I knew, I was being hoisted over his shoulder, causing me to yelp loudly. "You ass!"

"Hmmm, now this is an ass," he laughed as he slapped mine hard enough that it echoed throughout the room.

"Shhhh! I'm not ready for these idiots to know about us. I want to stay in this perfect bubble we've made for ourselves."

He set me down in the en suite. "Perfect, huh?"

I rolled my eyes. "You're so annoying."

"You love it," he teased and then turned on the shower.

"What are you doing?" I yelped when he pulled off his pants. My eyes immediately zeroed in on his impressive and half-hard again cock.

"*We* are getting cleaned up. Now strip."

"What happened to keeping our clothes on?"

"That was before I nutted in my pants like a teenager." His laugh made my chest feel funny. Most things he did made me feel things I wasn't accustomed to feeling.

Since I had just had the orgasm that I'd been waiting months for, I figured I was less likely to jump his bones, and being naked never bothered me, so I figured, *what the hell*, and pulled my shirt up over my head.

His eyes briefly focused on my chest before he turned to test the shower temperature. And then, in one of the many *fuck it* moments I'd had since we started seeing each other again, I decided to just go with it. I moved past him and into the shower. *It was just a shower. No big deal. Two adults can shower together.*

Brandon stepped in behind me, brushed my hair over my shoulder, and leaned in to place a kiss on my neck. "Good girl."

I spun and placed my hands on his chest. "Absolutely not."

His chuckle, paired with the accompanying handsome smile, almost did me in, but I held my ground. "You cannot be *good girling* me while we're doing this whole no-sex thing. It's not fair," I whined. "I only have so much willpower here, Brando."

His hand gripped my neck as he brought his face close to mine. "Okay, Sweetheart. Whatever you say." His other hand moved behind me to retrieve the body wash. "Now, let's get you cleaned up. I don't want to be responsible for your UTI."

I held out a hand and deposited a healthy amount of body wash into my palm. As I began lathering it up in my hands, Brandon did the same. Then this motherfucker started washing *me*. His hands slid over the curves of my body easily, but I was so focused on the feel of his hands on me that the body wash in my hands was quickly forgotten. I turned my back to him, and his hands moved to massage my shoulders. I groaned.

"Feel good?" he asked, increasing the pressure slightly.

"So good," I practically moaned.

"Careful," he warned. "I only have so much willpower, too, Sweetheart." His erection slid against my ass, causing me to push back into him.

36

BRANDON

exi's whole body was covered in soap. The feel of her slippery skin against mine was too much to bear. I wanted to bury myself inside her and never come out. She moaned as I massaged her shoulders. *Great, there goes my dick again.* I was so easily aroused by her. Literally everything she did was sexy as hell to me, but this. *This shower. Bubbles dripping down her slick skin and sliding against me?* I pressed my erection against her back, my willpower hanging by a thread.

I reached around her and massaged soap over her breasts and down her stomach, stopping before reaching the apex of her thighs. She ground herself into my touch and then turned to face me with more body wash in her hands.

Her soapy hands moved tentatively over my body, washing my chest and then my arms. She wasn't looking at me, though, so I tipped her chin up towards me. "You okay?"

She gave me a tight smile. "Yeah, I'm okay. But why are we waiting again?"

"Because you have an aversion to intimacy, remember?"

She chuckled, "Oh, yeah."

"And you revert to sex whenever things get too emotional."

"Mmmhmm." She continued to slather soap over my chest and abs.

"But you're doing so well. You've made a lot of progress, Lexi, and I'm proud of you." I rubbed my thumb over her pouty lip.

"But good girls get orgasms, right?"

Sneaky girl. "Yes, they do, but you've already had one tonight." I moved her back into the spray of the shower. "Now, I'm going to wash your hair, rinse you off, and then put you to bed."

Her pout intensified. "Rude. But you're right. We should wait a little longer. Although I must say, I've been having a lot of fun with you… even with our clothes on."

I leaned down to kiss her nose. "Good. Me too."

I REALLY WAS SO proud of Lexi. Sure, we were both itching to have sex again, but I didn't really think it was sex that was the problem. I believed the real test for her was in those intimate moments after sex when she'd usually run for the hills. Over the last month, she and I had gotten closer, more intimate, and it had nothing to do with sex. I think she realized that, and I was excited for us to get back home and keep building that trust.

I woke up the next morning to the sound of Christmas music playing throughout the cabin and the clanking of plates coming from downstairs. I groaned and stretched in bed. This bed was definitely not big enough for me, and I'd be sure to relay that feedback to my brother. Although I hoped that during future visits I'd be sharing the guest room with Lexi.

Speaking of Lexi, her laugh traveled up the stairs and engulfed me like a warm breeze. I loved her laugh. Smiling to myself, I heard a throat clear and turned my head to see Dylan eyeballing me. He raised an eyebrow. "You're ridiculous."

"Such a cynic." I tossed a pillow at him as I got out of bed. "You'll get it one day."

"Nah, I'm good, bro." Dylan snickered.

"Come on, sleepyheads," Daphne called from downstairs. "Breakfast is ready!"

"Coming!" I hollered down in response. "Come on, dickhead, let's go eat," I said to Dylan, pulling a shirt over my head.

As we came down the stairs, Daphne, Nathan, and Lexi were gathered at the kitchen island. Lexi looked up and greeted me with a huge smile that had me wanting to cross the room and give her a proper greeting. I couldn't wait until we could tell everyone that we were together.

"Morning," I greeted the group.

"Morning. I hope you're hungry; Daphne made enough to feed the whole town," Nathan joked.

"Har. Har. Our parents are coming too." Daphne rolled her eyes and turned to get something out of the oven. "Come on, guys, grab a plate."

"Well, if they don't show, I'm sure I can put a dent in this. It smells amazing, Daphne," I said as I picked up a plate. She didn't have to tell me twice. I was starving.

We all filled our plates and sat down to eat as my dad and Daphne's parents walked through the front door. We exchanged hurried greetings while stuffing our faces.

AFTER BREAKFAST, it was time for our Secret Santa gift exchange. Nathan rigged it so he'd get Daphne, so he could reveal a secret project he'd been working on since they met. He had written their love story and had it bound for her—an incredibly romantic gesture, Daphne was absolutely over the moon about. Daphne launched herself into Nathan's arms and sobbed into his neck. As I glanced over at Lexi, I noticed—*was she crying?* The urge to go to her was strong, but I remained in my seat across the room.

Lexi swiped a tear from her cheek and cleared her throat. "Okay, enough of that mushy shit. Jesus, Nate Dog, you're making men everywhere look bad."

After a few chuckles, Daphne peeled herself away from Nathan's embrace. "Okay, I'll go next. Dane, I had you," she said, retrieving a gift from under the tree.

When it was Lexi's turn to pass out her gift, she stood and picked up a gift from under the tree, and brought it to me. "I had you, Brando," she said casually as she handed me a neatly wrapped package.

"Thanks, Lexi." I ripped the paper to reveal a beautifully embossed, leather-bound sketchbook. It was like the one she'd gotten for my dad last year, but I could tell that this one was picked out or made especially for me. And it looked like the tentacles that adorned it were intricately carved by hand. My mouth hung open as I absentmindedly traced the design with a finger.

"Do you like it?" she asked.

I looked up to see everyone staring at me. "I love it," I answered her honestly. This was one of the most thoughtful gifts I'd ever received, and it meant even more because I knew how hard it was for Lexi to give such a heartfelt gift to me. I stood and gave her a half-hug that wouldn't seem out of the ordinary to anyone else. "Thank you. It's perfect."

Lexi went back to her seat, and the gifting continued around me, but I was still focused on the sketchbook. Because truthfully, it felt like more than a sketchbook— more than just a gift. It felt as if Lexi was telling me she cared in her own way. This was a romantic gesture, and I was here for it. Inside, I found a handwritten note, but quickly stuffed it back inside and closed the book. I'd have to read it away from prying eyes, but if she kept this up, I don't know if I'd be able to keep our secret for much longer.

The rest of the morning passed in a blur, but at the first moment I could, I snuck away back to the loft to read the note from Lexi.

Brandon,

As you know, I'm not great at expressing my feelings, but I want to be better, not only for you, but for myself. I didn't think I'd be able to say this to your face, so I wanted you to know… I really like you and care about you. I'm glad we're dating, or whatever this is, and getting to know each other more. I've been having a lot of fun with you these past weeks, and I'm excited to see where it will go. You were right when you said the post-sex intimacy is what scares me. The fear of falling for you, and then potentially losing you, terrifies me. So, please know that I'm trying. I won't ever be a super romantic person like you are, but I promise I will talk to you about what I'm feeling, and I won't run away again.

xoxo, Your Lexi

I reread it twice. This felt incredibly meaningful, especially coming from Lexi. *My* Lexi. Her note gave me hope that we were moving in the right direction and that she and I had a real shot at a future together. I tucked the note back into the sketchbook and made my way back downstairs. Lexi needed a proper thank you, and I was determined to give it to her.

37

LEXI

I was so nervous giving Brandon his gift in front of everyone. I wasn't sure he'd be able to keep his emotions under wraps. Or maybe I secretly hoped he wouldn't. I didn't know what I thought anymore. This time last year, I wouldn't have even entertained the idea of a relationship with anyone, and now I was dating my best friend's boyfriend's brother. *Say that ten times fast.*

Bundled up in a blanket, sitting by the roaring outdoor fireplace, I was lost in thought. I actually couldn't wait until our little secret was revealed. I just didn't want to tell everyone while we were stuck in this cabin. It would be too awkward. I'd much rather it came out when we got home, and we wouldn't have to field questions and scrutiny from all sides. At least at home, we could manage the fallout one-on-one.

"Hey," Brandon said, startling me.

"Shit! Hey yourself. I didn't hear you come out. How long were you standing there, you creeper?" I joked.

Brandon's smile warmed me. "Not long. Are you warm enough?"

"Yeah, it's not too cold today."

"Want to go for a walk?" he asked.

"In the snow?" I looked at him as if he'd lost his mind.

"Like you said, it's not too cold today. Don't worry, I'll keep you warm, Sweetheart." He arched an eyebrow.

I quickly scanned the wall of windows directly in front of us. Thankfully, no one was paying us any attention. "Okay, I guess, but if I get frostbite, I'm holding you personally responsible."

"Come on." He held his hand out to me, which I ignored. I got up and pulled the blanket tightly around myself, and walked down the porch stairs as Brandon trailed behind me. I gave one more look over my shoulder to make sure no one was watching us.

As soon as we were out of eyeshot, I looked towards Brandon as we walked side by side along the beach. "So, what's up?"

"I read your note."

"Fuck." I pulled the blanket up over my face. This was exactly why I wrote him a note—so I wouldn't have to actually talk about it.

Brandon pulled the blanket down and turned me to face him. "Look at me." Looking up into his eyes, I knew I could trust him with my heart. It was a weird and unfamiliar sensation, knowing that without a shadow of a doubt that he wouldn't intentionally hurt me. "Thank you. I know that wasn't easy for you to write, but I appreciate you telling me how you're feeling. And that sketchbook? Fucking perfect."

"You're welcome. Remember last year at the Christmas market when I got that sketchbook for your dad?"

"Yeah, that was really nice."

"Well, I went back this year and asked if he did custom pieces." My eyes drifted away from his. "So you like it?"

He tipped my chin up so I couldn't avoid his eyes. "I love it. Thank you."

"You're welcome."

He leaned down and whispered in my ear, "I like you too, Sweetheart."

"Oh, my God. Let's not make a big deal about the note, okay?" I tried to pull out of his grasp, but he held both of my arms to my sides.

"I know it's hard for you to talk about your feelings, but that note was really nice. Your opening up to me, even in a note, means the world to me. I want you to know that you're safe with me. Your heart is safe with me."

"Thank you," I replied, barely above a whisper. He was saying all the right things, but inside, I was having a mini freak-out. I wanted to give him more reassurance, but I wasn't sure I'd be able to describe adequately how I was feeling. Without meeting his eyes, I tried. "Trust isn't something I give people lightly, but I do trust you. I know I'm safe with you, and I promise I'll try to talk to you about how I'm feeling more."

"That's all I can ask for." He raised my hand to his mouth, kissing it briefly, before we continued our walk.

Brandon was going to ruin me for any other man. I hoped he wouldn't break my heart, but at that moment, I honestly trusted he wouldn't. I knew there were no guarantees in life, and I needed to be okay with that in order for us to move forward. After a few minutes, we rounded a bend and came to a small, more secluded beach. Tugging his hand, which was still in mine, I led him towards the wooded area. I wanted him. I wanted to stop pretending that sex was my issue. The realization that he wouldn't hurt me had me wanting to give myself to him without shying away afterwards. Once we were inside the cover of the woods, he pressed me against a tree.

"What are you doing, Sweetheart?" he asked with a wicked grin.

"I think we've waited long enough," I said breathlessly.

"And you think this is the best place for us to break our little vow of celibacy?" he chuckled as he looked from side to side.

"We're grown ass adults, Brandon, and it's not like we haven't had a ton of sex already. And besides, you know it's not the actual sex that's my issue." I wasn't above begging at that point. I was wound so damn tight. "Don't you think I've made some good progress? I think I deserve a reward."

He pressed into me so I could feel how much he wanted me, too. "You know I want you. I always want you, but I want more than just your body, Lexi. Do I have that?"

"Yes," I breathed as he captured my mouth with his.

"Promise me if you feel like running, you'll talk to me."

"I promise. Please fuck me—I'm pretty sure my hymen has grown back."

"Oh my God, Lex." His chuckle tickled my ear. "I don't have any condoms." His hands moved over my body inside the blanket.

"Brando, I haven't ever not used a condom, and on top of that, I was tested months ago, and we've already established the fact that I am a born-again virgin. I'm good—please put me out of my misery."

"I haven't been with anyone else either. Are you sure?" I could tell from his tone, he was struggling to maintain control.

"Yes," I said, pulling him into a kiss. I palmed his cock through his sweatpants—a silent plea for him to take me right there.

"I should make you wait, make you beg—" He spun me hurriedly, pressing my front against the tree. With his face next to mine, he reached between my legs to cup my pussy that was begging to be filled. "—but I've already waited too long to claim what's mine again."

"Do it. Fuck me."

38

BRANDON

My restraint disintegrated. *Did I really want our first time back with each other to be up against a tree in the woods in the middle of winter?* Truthfully, I had planned on making it special, but that wasn't Lexi's style; it wasn't us. Our entire relationship had been spontaneous and fun, not slow and romantic. Even though I was a romantic at heart and wanted to do romantic things for her—and I would in time—I knew that this was actually the perfect way for us to reconnect sexually. Impulsively and full of passion. Lexi had shown me she was in this for the right reasons, and I had to trust she wouldn't run again if we crossed this line.

I stepped back to pull the blanket off of her, tossing it onto a nearby tree log. "Don't worry, Sweetheart, I'll make sure you stay warm."

"Yeah, fuck that blanket. I'm on fire. Please, Brandon, I need you to touch me."

I pulled her leggings and thong down in one motion. Then I put my arm around her waist to pull her away from the tree, and used my other hand to push her back down flat. "Hold on to the tree, Lexi."

She yelped but complied, arching her back so her beautiful ass was just where I wanted it. I kicked her legs out, stretching her leggings to their limit, and then squatted behind her. Running my hands over her smooth skin, I took my time teasing her. She wriggled against my touch, wordlessly begging for more. "Ut-ah," I tutted. "Patience, Sweetheart."

"I swear to Christ, Brandon, if you pull that edging crap right now out here in the snow, I'm going to murder you and leave your corpse to rot." I laughed, because what else could I do? Lexi always said the most unhinged shit. I loved that about her. *Shit*. I knew I had the potential to fall for her, but the last few weeks really had me envisioning a future with her. We fit together so well despite our differences. It hit me like a freight train—I was in love with her, and I think I had been for a long time. But I was definitely not ready to let that slip out.

Instead, I spread her ass cheeks with my hands and buried my face between her legs. I swiped my tongue over her clit, through her slick pussy lips, and then over and around her tight little asshole. Lexi hissed, "Yessss!"

She was so wet already, but I needed her sopping before I gave her what we were both so desperate for. I continued to lap at her center as she mewled her approval and writhed against me. I pushed two fingers into her, causing her to gasp. "You okay, Sweetheart?" My other hand reached around her to pinch her clit.

"Yes, fuck, that feels so good. I need more. I need you. Please," she begged as I continued to finger fuck her.

"I want you to come on my face first, and then I'll let you come on my cock." Picking up my pace, I could feel that she was getting close. I removed my fingers from her pussy and replaced them with my tongue as I continued my clitoral assault with my other hand.

"I'm so close. Don't stop."

I kept the same pressure and speed with my fingers and continued fucking her with my tongue until she tightened around me and came hard, soaking my face as she did. *Mission accomplished.*

I stood quickly and pulled my painfully hard erection from my pants. Rubbing the head of my cock over her still throbbing clit, I leaned down and asked, "You still want this?"

"Yes," she moaned. "Please. I need this."

"I've missed this—missed you. So much," I croaked as I unhurriedly nudged inside of her.

"God, I almost forgot how big you are," Lexi breathed.

I paused my forward motion. "Are you okay?"

"I'm fine, really, just move. Please, I need you." Whether or not she meant it the way I heard it, it didn't matter. Hearing her say she needed me in any capacity lit a fire in me.

"Baby, hold on." I gradually pushed the rest of the way into her, stretching her as I did. "Fuck, Lexi. The sight of your pussy stretched around me bare—holy fuck," I groaned. I'd never fucked anyone without a condom, and having this experience for the first time with Lexi just felt right.

After taking a moment to appreciate the feel of her fully wrapped around me, I started to move in long, deliberate thrusts. Her hands moved further up the tree, changing the angle enough so I was even deeper. "Yes, oh God, yes. I missed this. Fuck me. Hard. Please."

And I did. I increased my pace, and Lexi cried out her appreciation. We were a mess of grunts and groans; the sounds of our bodies slick with sweat slapping together echoed throughout our private alcove. I wanted this to last forever, but we were out in the cold, and I wasn't going to last long anyway. It had been too damn long. But first, I needed her to come again, so I reached around to apply pressure to her clit.

"Mmmhmm. Just like that. Fuck, Brandon, I'm gonna come," she moaned. I felt her tighten around me, sending me over the edge, too. My upper body folded onto hers as we both rode out the aftermath of our release. "God, I needed that," Lexi chuckled.

I grinned against her back. "Yeah, me too. Although I don't know if anything will ever beat coming in my pants like a horny teenager last night."

She laughed loudly. "Oh shit, yeah, that was pretty hot."

I pulled out of her and leaned down to pull her leggings back into place.

She batted at my hands. "Wait, let me find a leaf or something to clean up."

"A leaf? That can't be hygienic. I thought you were a nurse." I finished pulling her pants up and then tucked myself back into my sweatpants.

She slapped my arm. "I'm a mess. I need something to clean up. Give me your sleeve."

"Nope," I said, popping the P. "I want you to go back to the cabin with me dripping out of you."

"Neanderthal." She rolled her eyes.

"But I'm your Neanderthal," I said, leaning down and capturing her mouth with mine.

39

—————

LEXI

I kissed Brandon back, but it felt different. It felt as if I were kissing him for the first time. I know, but as corny as that sounds, it was true. I had worked so hard to let him in and open myself up to the possibility of a future with him. The no-sex pact was stupid. I knew that wasn't my issue, but it was the only thing I could think of to give us a fresh start. And now that we'd crossed that line again, I was determined to show Brandon that I wouldn't fall into old habits.

Brandon broke our kiss and retrieved my discarded blanket. After wrapping it tightly around me, he looked me in the eyes. "Are you okay?"

I took his face in my hands, admiring his devilishly handsome features. "I'm great, really. Now let's try to sneak back into the cabin without getting caught."

"You look like you got fucked against a tree in the woods, so good luck with that," he laughed.

Taking him by the hand, I started leading him back. "It'll be fiiiine."

We walked hand in hand until the cabin came back into sight. I did my best to make sure my clothes were fully back in place and that we didn't actually look like two idiots who had just fucked in the woods.

"We look okay, right?" I asked Brandon as we approached the cabin.

"Yeah, but I don't see how we're gonna sneak in. The whole damn house is windows."

"We were out for a walk. Nothing suspicious. Just two people walking in the snow." *If I believed it, maybe everyone else would.*

"Yeah, that sounds totally believable. You seem pretty outdoorsy." Brandon's amused tone had me chuckling, too.

"Ass." I couldn't help but smile. I was actually happy and looking forward to getting home to continue exploring a relationship with Brandon.

Walking up the steps to the cabin's back porch, I couldn't see anyone inside. "Quick, go!" I whisper yelled at Brandon as I pushed him in front of me.

The house was quiet. *Did everyone leave?* It was Christmas Day, so nothing in town was open. It's not like they'd go for a drive either. *Weird.*

"Go upstairs," I said under my breath. "I'll go to my room and text Daphne to see where everyone is."

Before I could slink away, Brandon grabbed my hand and pulled me into an embrace. He grinned and pointed to the mistletoe above us before leaning in to kiss me gently on the lips. "See you soon, Sweetheart."

I pushed away from him as I surveyed the room for prying eyes, but no one was there. "I'm going to murder you. Remember, I found the perfect spot to hide your body."

Brandon snickered and then took the stairs two at a time to get to the loft. Once I was safely in the guestroom, I grabbed my phone to text Daphne, but found a text from her instead.

DAPHNE

Hey, our parents went back to their cabin to relax before dinner, and Nathan and I are "napping." Hope you're having a nice "walk."

Mother fucker.

ME

We've been made. Daphne saw us sneaking off. The parents went back to their cabin, and Daphne is boning your brother. Where's Dylan?

BRANDON

TMI. Dylan's asleep up here.

ME

Good. That means the coast is clear. I'm going to take a shower and wash this cum off me. Meet me in the living room after.

BRANDON

I like my cum on you. In you. I can't wait to paint those beautiful tits with it, too.

Oof. The mouth on this man.

I showered quickly and met him in the living room, taking a seat on the floor next to the crackling fireplace. I opened the hutch next to me and asked, "Wanna play a game?"

"Sure. What did you have in mind?"

I pulled out the perfect game, holding it up next to my smiling face, and batted my eyes at him.

A laugh burst out of him as the door to Daphne and Nathan's room opened. "What are you two up to?" Daphne asked as she joined us by the fire.

Brandon shook his head. "Playing Sorry, apparently."

THE NEXT MORNING, I packed up to head back to the city. Daphne and Nathan were staying for a few more days and offered for me to stay, but I didn't want to intrude on their love fest. Besides, I was itching to get home and have some non-outdoorsy time with my man. *Who was I even?*

Daphne's parents had already taken off earlier, and Dane was waiting in the living room for Brandon and Dylan to finish packing. I was sitting at the kitchen island chatting with Daphne when the boys came stomping down the stairs.

Damn, Brandon looked good. He was even wearing that

damn Santa hat he knew did something to me. He had worn it the night before after dinner, too, for which I may have sent him a dirty text after I went to my room to go to bed. We didn't sneak off again, though. We decided to save it for when we got home so he could *'punish me properly for making him wait so long'* or whatever. *Insert eye roll.*

Once we were all packed and ready to go, we went outside to warm up and load our cars. After saying our goodbyes and doling out hugs, I got in my car and rolled down the window. "Hey, everyone!" I shouted and they all turned to look at me. "Brando and I are dating! Byyyyyyyy-eeee!" And then peeled out of the driveway.

EPILOGUE
LEXI

It had been weeks since I dropped that bomb at the cabin, but as it turned out it wasn't much of a bomb. Dylan and Daphne already knew, and Dane and Nathan weren't all that surprised. I believe Brandon said, '*They were like, yeah, no shit*' or something like that. I guess we hadn't been as sneaky as we thought. Whatever, it was still fun to secretly date while it lasted.

The bell above the door to the shop announced my arrival, and Paige looked up to greet me. "Hey, Lexi. Go ahead back."

"Thanks, girl. Love that top." Over the past few weeks, I'd gotten to know Paige pretty well and had a feeling she and I were going to be good friends. *Look at me making friends and shit!*

"Thanks! I just got it," she smiled up at me as I passed her.

"Hey, Brando," I cooed.

Brandon immediately stood and lifted me into a hug. "There's my girl! I missed you," he said, burying his face in my neck, making me chuckle. I couldn't believe how far we'd come. "How was work?" he asked as he set me back down.

"Not too bad, I guess. I mean, it was work, so…" I snickered. "How about you?"

"Pretty good. I'm finishing my girlfriend's tattoo today, so that's pretty cool." Before I could respond with some smartass comment, he leaned down and kissed me. I smiled against his lips. Dating Brandon was not at all what I'd expected. Initially, I thought he'd be super clingy and annoyingly romantic, but it was almost as if he knew exactly what I needed in a partner. Or maybe we were actually meant to be. *Ha!* I was still me. I wasn't about to start believing in fate all of a sudden. Truthfully, we balanced each other out so well. He pushed me to talk about my feelings, and I coaxed him into being more adventurous. He was funny and kind, made me feel safe and loved, but still fucked me within an inch of my life just about every day. You could say things were going pretty well.

A throat cleared behind me. "Hey, I'm gonna get out of here," Paige said, interrupting our kiss. "I'll lock up. You kids have fun."

"Thanks, Paige. See ya tomorrow," Brandon called after her.

"Bye!" I gave a small wave and then moved to sit on Brandon's table. Swinging my legs, I teased, "All alone. Whatever will we do?"

"Finish your tattoo," Brandon said seriously.

"Boo, you're no fun," I pouted and crossed my arms over my chest.

"You know that's not true. Now, don't be a brat, and you'll get your reward when we get home." *Home.* He said that often. While we didn't share a home, whenever he'd slip and say that, my heart skipped a beat. Okay, I knew I wasn't actually having palpitations. *I'm a nurse, duh,* but I would get a funny feeling in my chest. It was a feeling that until recently had been unfamiliar to me.

He moved to put the privacy screen in place. Even though it was only the two of us in the shop for the rest of the evening, he wanted to make sure I wouldn't be exposed if his brother or dad stopped by unexpectedly.

As soon as it was in place, I stood and peeled off my pants slowly, making eye contact with him the entire time. I knew we were just going to finish my tattoo, but it was too fun messing with him. "Behave, Sweetheart," he said with an arched eyebrow and handed me a sheet to cover myself. The heat in his eyes gave him away. I knew the effect I had on him because it was the same effect he had on me—and not just sexually. Some of our most fun times had actually been while we'd been fully clothed. *Wild, I know.*

I wrapped the sheet around myself and hopped back up onto the table. "Okay, Buzz Killington. Let's get this show on the road, then."

Brandon chuckled as he readied his supplies. When I'd left town, my tattoo was only half done. I hadn't been in a hurry to finish it since I got back, but it finally felt like it was time. Brandon and I were in a good place, the cat was out of the bag about our relationship, and I was ready to finally let go of my past. Finishing my tattoo felt like the logical next step.

"So, did you mail that letter this morning?" Brandon asked as he started cleaning my leg. Mother fucker liked to ask me uncomfortable questions while I couldn't go anywhere, like now or while tied to his bed.

"I did."

"And how are you feeling about it?"

"Fine."

"Lexi—" His tone let me know I wouldn't get out of talking about this.

"I'm okay, really. I think I was more emotional after I finished writing it. Dropping it in the mail wasn't too bad." I sighed. "I'm glad it's done."

"I'm proud of you, Sweetheart," he said with nothing but admiration in his voice.

"I'm proud of myself, too, actually," I said honestly, because I was proud of myself. In therapy, I came to terms with the fact that I actually had been pushing people away because of my own abandonment issues, rather than my not wanting to end up like my mom. Apparently, those were two different things, and I'd been projecting my own issues onto my mom. Then, after months of therapy and working on myself, I finally felt the weight of my father's abandonment lifting. My therapist suggested I write him a letter to gain some sort of closure. While I fought the idea tooth and nail at first, as time went on and I got stronger, I felt like it was the best thing I could do for myself. It wasn't for him because, fuck that guy. But I deserved closure, and this was the only way I could get it without talking to him face to face, which would not be on any of my Bingo cards, ever.

Turned out he was in prison yet again, but that time in Arizona. He caught another drug charge and would be incarcerated for the foreseeable future. The thought of going to see him in prison never even crossed my mind. He didn't deserve my time or energy. I went through every emotion as I wrote the letter—sadness, anger, guilt, relief. But I also felt an immense sense of pride after I'd finished it. I didn't put a return address, and he had no way of responding to me, but getting all the things I had to say to him off my chest felt like a huge relief. Even if he never got it or read it, I had the closure I needed to move forward with my life and with Brandon. *Brandon,* who was emotionally available and wanted to give me everything I'd never had from a man in my life before—*stability, hope, love.*

"You doing okay, Lexi?" Brandon asked, pulling me back into the present, the hum of his machine still buzzing as he worked.

"I'm good. Just thinking."

"Want to share with the class?" he chuckled.

"I love you."

EPILOGUE TWO
BRANDON

I t had been months since finishing Lexi's tattoo—*after she told me she loved me*. We were still together, and I'd never been happier. Hearing her say those words both shocked and moved me, especially since I never imagined she'd be the one to say it first. Fucking Lexi never failed to surprise me. I loved her then with every fiber of my being, and still do. I tell her every single day without fail. *Was our meeting fate?* If you asked Lexi, she'd still laugh in your face, but I wasn't so sure. Whether we met through Daphne and Nathan or at The Basement on a random night, I think she was always meant to be mine and I hers, and I plan on spending the rest of my days showing her how grateful I am for her existence.

I smiled to myself as I looked around the table. Sunday dinners at my dad's place were a little more of a rowdy affair these days. Daphne, Nathan, Lexi, Dylan, Dad, and I were all laughing at something Coco was doing to the wall. That cat was nuts and actually pretty entertaining.

I reached my hand under the table to squeeze Lexi's thigh. Without looking in my direction, she smiled and placed her hand over mine.

"So when are you two tying the knot? You're not getting any younger." Lexi's eyes grew slightly wider, and her grip on my hand intensified until she realized my dad's question was directed towards Nathan and Daphne. I chuckled and patted her leg.

"We're not in any hurry, Dad. We're just enjoying each other's company for now," Nathan answered for them.

"You kids these days, never in a hurry for anything," he sighed.

"Okay, Gramps." Dylan laughed. "You're not even that old, Dad. Quit acting like an old man."

"So sue me for wanting my kids happy and settled down. I don't know what you're all waiting for. Life's too short."

He was right; life was too short, but like Nathan and Daphne, Lexi and I were taking things slow. We didn't even have any plans to move in together yet, although we rarely stayed apart anymore.

As if on cue, Coco jumped into Dad's lap and started rubbing her face all over him and purring her little heart out. "I guess Coco Baby will be my only grandbaby," he cooed.

"Yeah, that's definitely the only one you'll ever get from me," Dylan announced.

Nathan piped up next. "I hope you eat your words one day, brother."

Dylan arched his eyebrow. "Wanna put money on it?"

AFTER DINNER and our after-dinner routine of shooting the shit in the back room, it was time to call it a night. Lexi and I said our goodbyes and followed Dylan out to our cars. Coco pranced beside us, showing off her new leash and harness set. Lexi was making a fuss over her while I chatted with Dylan about some work nonsense.

"Yeah, I can be there—" Dylan trailed off as something caught his eye down the street.

"You okay?" I asked, following his line of sight.

"What's happening at the Davies' place?" His furrowed brow grew deeper. "Is he moving?"

"I'm not sure. I haven't seen anyone over there in a while, but I think Mr. Davies passed away recently."

"He's dead?" he asked with what sounded like concern in his voice.

"I think so. If I remember correctly, Dad mentioned it last week." I was getting concerned myself. I wasn't sure why Dylan would even care.

Dylan was frantically looking at the Davies' home. He appeared to be searching for something. Then he froze.

"No fucking way," he said under his breath. He then

dropped Coco's leash and took off towards the Davies' house.

Want more spice from Brandon and Lexi? Scan the QR code below for an extra spicy bonus scene!

ABOUT THE AUTHOR

Michele Elizabeth is a romance author, coffee addict, and certified crazy cat lady with a flair for turning everyday chaos into the kind of spicy, swoon-worthy stories you can't put down. Married to her real-life book boyfriend and surrounded by four furballs with attitude, she somehow balances writing with wrangling real life in sunny Southern California—and loves every messy second of it.

After starting her own spicy book group, she fell hard for steamy reads, and now writes her own—raw, real, character-driven stories packed with heart, heat, and just enough rough edges to keep it authentic.

By night, she works as an operating room nurse. By every other moment, she's crafting romances that'll keep you up past your bedtime.

Be sure to follow along for updates!

@michelewritesromance
on Amazon, Goodreads, FB, IG & TikTok

Check out MicheleElizabeth.com to sign up for her newsletter and to get first access to her new releases, events, and other news.

ACKNOWLEDGMENTS

To my husband–Thank you again for always encouraging me to follow my dreams. Thank you for being my sounding board and rock while I struggled through edits. And thank you for helping me "workshop" certain scenes... for science.

To Alicia–Thank you for being the Lexi to my Daphne. Thank you for being available to FaceTime at all hours to help me work through plot points, ramble endlessly, and then ultimately do what I was going to do anyway. I know I'm a pain in the ass sometimes, but you wouldn't want me any other way.

To my beta readers–Valeria, Justine, Katarina, Erika, Jessica, Tanya, and Kimberly your unhinged commentary gave me fucking LIFE! Thank you for your honesty and candor. You made the final version of *Snowbody Has to Know* something I'm truly proud of.

To my street team—aka The Smut Scouts—Thank you for helping hype up my books and being a safe space for me to share all of my crazy thoughts and ideas! Love you all!

Check out www.MicheleElizabeth.com to sign up for her newsletter and to get first access to her new releases, bonus chapters, events, and other news.

www.ingramcontent.com/pod-product-compliance
Lightning Source LLC
Chambersburg PA
CBHW071542110726
47908CB00007B/1968